THE WAY OF A TEXAN

THE WAY OF A TEXAN

Walt Coburn

CHIVERS
THORNDIKE

This Large Print edition is published by BBC Audiobooks Ltd, Bath, England and by Thorndike Press®, Waterville, Maine, USA.

Published in 2003 in the U.K. by arrangement with the author c/o Golden West Literary Agency.

Published in 2003 in the U.S. by arrangement with Golden West Literary Agency.

U.K. Hardcover   ISBN 0–7540–7380–7   (Chivers Large Print)
U.K. Softcover   ISBN 0–7540–7381–5   (Camden Large Print)
U.S. Softcover   ISBN 0–7862–5678–8   (Nightingale)

Copyright © 1953 by Star Guidance, Inc.

All rights reserved.

The text of this Large Print edition is unabridged.
Other aspects of the book may vary from the original edition.

Set in 16 pt. New Times Roman.

Printed in Great Britain on acid-free paper.

British Library Cataloguing in Publication Data available

Library of Congress Cataloging-in-Publication Data

Coburn, Walt, 1889–1971.
    The way of a Texan / Walt Coburn.
       p.   cm.
    ISBN 0–7862–5678–8 (lg. print : sc : alk. paper)
    1. Mexico—Fiction. 2. Large type books. I. Title.
PS3505.O153W39 2003
813'.52—dc21   2003055976

ESSEX COUNTY COUNCIL
LIBRARIES

CHAPTER ONE

Bass McCoy's six-root, rawboned frame filled the doorway of a cantina in the Mexican section of Laredo, Texas. It was Sunday morning, and Bass had been waiting there since sunrise for his father, Captain Clay McCoy of the Texas Rangers. The bullet-torn body of the stranger Bass had shot to death in a drunken ruckus the night before lay covered by a dirty old tarpaulin in a far corner of the now-deserted cantina.

Bass had found a Texas Ranger commission sewn in the neckband of the dead man's shirt, and he knew he would be charged with murder, regardless of the circumstances, for killing a Texas Ranger on Texas soil. He could have pulled out after the killing and crossed the Rio Grande into Mexico, but it was not in the nature of Bass to run away from anything. He was waiting to be arrested for the killing.

The rotgut Bass had swilled down the preceding night was dead in his system, and his empty belly crawled with nausea that kept coming up into his throat. There was the clammy feeling of cold, sick sweat that kept breaking out from every pore, as waves of nausea swept over him. His coarse black hair under his low-brimmed hat was dank, and a grayish pallor showed under the wiry stubble of a two-day growth of whiskers. His eyes were bloodshot gray slits as they squinted into the rising sun to watch the deserted street.

Burro Alley was lined on either side by unpainted adobe huts, cantinas and brothels, the doors of which were now shut and the blinds pulled low. It was drab and ugly by daylight when Burro Alley slept off its booze. Only under the cover of darkness did the sordid, crooked street on the north bank of the Rio Grande come alive.

The street was empty now and silent, dead as the corpse inside the filthy cantina, empty as the bottles, half-buried in the heavy dust of the alley, but Bass knew that more than one pair of eyes inside the adobe jacals were peering through cracks, watching him as he stood in the doorway, waiting. Folks were uneasy, knowing the wrath of Captain Clay McCoy, admiring in their fear the guts it took for young Bass to stay to meet his Ranger father, a fearsome man, whose name struck terror even into the toughest renegade heart.

Six days a week the Ranger Captain buckled on his guns to attend to his duties. Cold-blooded, steel-nerved, slow to anger, they said of the Ranger Captain that he never pulled a gun without using it, and he never shot to miss. Unlike most killers, he never talked about it afterward.

Sundays he left his guns at home and put on a carefully-brushed, rusty-black clawhammer coat and a boiled shirt. He put the Bible, that had been carried for years by his circular-riding father, in the tail pocket of the coat, saddled his blue mule and rode to church or camp meeting along the river bank. McCoy was a deacon in the church. No man had ever heard him laugh.

Bass had no memory of any mother, only a series of work-worn Mexican women who had kept house for the Ranger. When Bass was a kid, his father had made him dress in his Sunday clothes and ride astride the blue mule, behind him in the saddle, to camp meetings. To the boy's way of thinking, his father enforced religion on Sundays like he enforced the laws of Texas on week-days, so that the laws of Texas and the Ten Commandments became as one. Bass grew up in open defiance of both.

The McCoy ranch lay a few miles down the river from Laredo, and Bass had done a man's work on it since he could remember. He figured he owed nothing to his Bible-toting father. What money he was paid for the ranch work, Bass squandered in typical cowboy fashion when he came to town, like he had done yesterday.

Bass had done a good job of town-painting this past night and had wound up in the Mexican part of Laredo at a Saturday night baile. Bassito, the Mexicans called him, and they always made him welcome, drunk or sober, and he had been drunker than seven hundred dollars last night.

His memory was fogged and hazy. He recalled dancing with a beautiful redheaded girl with amber eyes, who had refused to tell him her name. She was not Mexican so he had called her 'Gringita.' They had had every dance together, and then all of a sudden she was gone. Without her, the baile lost its flavor, so Bass had wandered into the dingy cantina that was crowded with ranch hands.

Then a big towheaded Texan had swaggered in, drunk and looking for trouble. He kept pawing the percentage girls who made their living cadging drinks, and Bass remembered how he had kept avoiding a run-in with him, because he knew that fighting a Texan in Burro Alley would mean trouble for his Mexican friends.

When the redheaded girl had come into the cantina and the big towhead had grabbed her, she had let out a thin cry. Then Bass could no longer restrain himself and knocked the obnoxious character down.

The gringo came up quickly with a gun in his hand, and Bass saw it spit flame. Bass, swift as lightning, had pulled his own gun. The big towheaded cowpuncher lay on the hard-packed dirt floor in a widening pool of blood.

Bass had stood there for a long time, the smoking gun in his hand, staring down at the man he had killed. When the drunken, blurred glaze went out of his eyes, and he finally looked around him, he was alone in the cantina with the dead stranger. The owner of the place had gone with the others, and there was no sign of the red-haired girl.

Bass knew that all he had to do was ride away from the scene. There would be nobody to tell Captain Clay McCoy that his son had killed a gringo stranger. No amount of questioning by the Texas law of the Mexicans who had witnessed the shooting would ever get a shred of information from any of them. Bass could sober up across the river and then go back to the ranch. The stink of the gringo killing would die out after a time. But that was not Bass McCoy's way.

By sunrise the news of the killing would reach the ears of the Ranger Captain, and Bass knew that his father would come. By now the Ranger Captain would know that Bass was waiting for him.

When Bass finally saw his father on the blue mule at the far end of the dingy alley, his belly muscles knotted, and the blood pounded in his throat.

When the Captain reached the cantina and pulled the mule up, the eyes of the two men met and held in a long silence. Then the Ranger Captain spoke. 'I'm giving you until Monday morning at sunrise to quit Texas.' He took a long, brown envelope from his coat pocket and shoved it into Bass' hand. Then he reined his mule and went back over the dusty street without once turning his head to look behind him.

Bass stared down at the brown envelope and the words written on it, in his father's handwriting. 'Bass McCoy. To be opened on his 21st Birthday.'

Bass had never celebrated a birthday, had never known the exact date of his birth. He lifted his head to stare after the Ranger Captain, but the mule and its rider were gone, leaving a dusty, drab haze.

The envelope became suddenly weighty, and sweat collected on the palms of his hands. His father had never given him a birthday present until now, and he dreaded breaking the seal. His hands were unsteady as he ripped the flap open and removed a single sheet of paper. On it was written:

'Today is your 21st birthday, and you have come into a man's stature. Therefore, it is your right to know the true facts regarding your heritage. I, Clay McCoy, am not your true flesh-and-blood father. Your father was an outlaw named Jim Slocum, one of the old Sam Bass gang. You were named in honor of their outlaw leader.

'Eighteen years ago I shot and killed your outlaw father on the main street of Laredo, Texas, in line of duty. Your mother died when you were born, and by killing your father, I had made you an orphan. I felt it my duty to adopt you and give you my name.

'I have tried, in my own way and according to my own lights, to raise you as if you were my own flesh-and-blood son; to live an honest, law-abiding and God-fearing life. In this I have failed.

'The news has just reached me that you have killed a man in a drunken brawl. Because I have failed in your upbringing, I take a goodly share of the blame for what you've done, and I will give you the chance to quit Texas.

'This day ends my guardianship over you. May God have mercy on you.' The letter was signed: 'Clay McCoy, Captain of the Texas Rangers.'

Bass crushed and twisted the paper in his hands, his eyes gun-metal, bloodshot and congested with bitterness. He was beginning to understand now the resentment that had grown into open rebellion within him against his Ranger father who had tried to cram his law and hidebound religion on a defenseless kid who had the wild, reckless blood of his outlaw father in his veins.

Bass pulled a match head along the seat of his pants and set the letter on fire, holding it until the last of the burning paper scorched his hand, closing his fist to crush the last white ashes.

'The psalm-shoutin', murderin' son-of-a-bitch!' Bass dusted the ashes from his hand

and headed down the street for the feed yard where he had left his horse. He saddled and headed for the river, crossing the Rio Grande into Mexico. He took the name of his outlaw father. He was Bass Slocum when his horse splashed ashore where some Mexicans were driving a small herd of cattle and lifting voice in the endless verses of 'La Cucaracha,' the marching song of Pancho Villa's rebel army.

'Bassito!' shouted a Mexican who recognized Bass.

'Amigo!' Bass replied and took a half-filled bottle from his saddlebag. Lifting it, he said, 'Salud!' Then he tilted the bottle, drank, and passed it to his friend.

The bottle glass caught the morning sun, as the man returned it, untouched, and Bass Slocum's slitted eyes were reflected there, hard and cold as splintered steel, the red veins like blood streaks on a gun barrel. Bass drank again to what lay behind him. Drank again to what lay ahead for a reckless, dangerous future. Bass Slocum had come into the heritage of his outlaw father . . .

* * *

Forty miles above Laredo, the three-house town of Palofox was the headquarters for the Texas Rangers, and directly across from Palofox in Mexico was the town of Hidalgo. Both towns were in a crooked arm of the Big

Bend of the Rio Grande.

With Texas involved with the rest of the United States in World War I, and with Mexico in the blood-spattered grip of a revolution, the border was far more dangerous than it had been since the battle of the Alamo. The Rio Grande river was the dividing line between Mexicans and Americans, as the hatred built up.

Prohibition made bootlegging a profitable business, and gun-running paid even better. The risk was high in proportion to the profits, and the only crime involved was getting caught with a load of tequila crossing into Texas, or a pack-load of guns going into Mexico.

The night Bass walked into the crowded cantina at Hidalgo, there was little left to identify the renegade Bass Slocum with Bass McCoy who had left Laredo a little over a year ago. Perhaps it was because of the black mustache that drooped down to cover the hardbitten corners of his mouth, or the sun-blackened texture of his skin and the deep lines etched around the corners of his gray eyes and their sharp, suspicious, hard scrutiny when he looked at a stranger. Or maybe it was his swagger.

Though Bass had been outlawed for about a year, he had aged ten years while he built up his tough reputation. He had hand-picked the dozen men who took his orders. Bass Slocum was alone now as he walked into the crowded cantina, unnoticed. He stepped aside from the swinging half-doors and stood against the wall. His eyes, adjusting to the smoky lamplight, took in every man there, a trick he had learned by way of self-preservation.

One man stood apart, head and shoulders above the rest, his back to the bar. He was a big man with sunburnt skin and a week's stubble of yellow whiskers. Crossed cartridge belts sagged around his waist, and the holsters that held a pair of pearl-handled six-shooters were tied down along each thick thigh. The man stood nearly seven feet, and his two hundred and fifty pounds were big bone and hard meat.

'Twenty-five mules in my pack train.' His voice was thick, guttural, as he talked to a heavy-set Mexican. 'They cross the river with tequila and return the same night with guns.' He lifted the bottle in his hand. 'And no damned Texican Ranger has the guts to stop Lobo Jones!' He bared his big teeth that clamped down across the neck of the bottle he tilted, and a hush came over the cantina.

'Aleman bastard!' Bass Slocum's Texas drawl fell across the silence.

The bottle jerked away, and the blond giant choked on the raw tequila, spewing it all over the Mexican's linen suit. The big man's florid face had a mottled look in the smoky lamplight.

Bass shoved away from the wall, and made

his way slowly toward the big man whose pale, small eyes looked murderous. Bass halted about ten feet away.

'Aleman. German bastard!' Bass repeated, his hand on his gun.

The crowd pushed back, all but the Mexican in the linen suit, who had sidestepped just enough to put himself out of the line of fire.

The big man still had the bottle in his hand that shook slightly now, while the color came back into his face. Bass saw the uncontrollable anger inside his opponent. It was not fear that made the giant's hand shake and send the blood into his face. It was hate and the lust to kill, mixed with the puzzlement that showed in his eyes.

'I got the message you sent me,' Bass said flatly. 'To throw in with you or get out of Mexico. I'm Bass Slocum, Texan. My men just hi-jacked your pack train loaded with guns.'

The knuckles of the big hand gripping the bottle showed bone-white. As the bottle lifted, Bass shot it from Lobo Jones' hand and stepped back, the smoking gun covering the Mexican in the linen suit along with the blond giant.

Jones was holding up his hand that was covered with blood, splinters of the shattered bottle showing through the torn flesh, his eyes staring at the maimed, bloody hand, the sweat breaking out on his face.

The place still held the echoes of the

explosion of the heavy-calibered gun. The acrid smell of burnt powder smoke was in the air.

Bass Slocum's eyes were slivers as they cut a hard look at the Mexican, and then fastened on the big gringo. 'Mexico is too small to hold both of us. It's your move, Aleman. Git!'

Bass followed the big man who lurched through the swinging doors. Bass had his gun in his hand, and his narrowed eyes cut quick-darting glances into the dark shadows as Lobo Jones forked the big black horse he had left tied to the hitchrack. Bass had his back flattened against the outer adobe wall of the cantina as he watched the big man spur off into the night.

'You made a big mistake.' A woman's husky voice came out of the shadows. 'Why didn't you kill him while you had him?' She stepped into the shaft of slim light that filtered from the doorway. 'You'll never get another chance,' she finished.

The woman was tall, angular. She looked impressive, even in her cowpuncher clothes and boots, a cartridge belt with a holstered gun slanted across her lean thighs. Her short-cut, thick, iron-gray hair showed under the old Stetson hat, slanted down across her black eyes that looked at him with keen appraisal. Her skin had a leathery texture, the lines etched deep around her eyes and the corners of her mouth. She was a handsome, striking-looking woman, despite the hardness stamped on her face. Her teeth showed very white as her lips peeled back in more of a grin than a smile. She cradled a short-barreled saddle carbine in her left arm and held out a slim, tanned hand.

'I'm Kate Crawford of the Big C outfit.' She spoke in a deep voice.

Bass pulled the hat from his sweat-matted black hair and wiped his perspiring right hand along the edge of his faded levis. Kate Crawford was almost a legendary person, and the Big C outfit in Texas and the Santa Catalina Grant in Mexico, a fabulous empire.

'You're Bass McCoy.' She gripped his hand.

'The name's Slocum. Bass Slocum,' Bass corrected her, his voice quiet.

'Slocum.' Her eyes narrowed a little. 'Have it your own way, Bass.' The smile thinned. 'I've been trying to cut your sign for more than a year.'

Bass stiffened a little and let go of her hand. 'Porque?' he asked bluntly.

'I want to hire you and your men. There's some horses and a lot of Big C cattle on this side of the line. I want you and your tough hands to trail them into Texas. My Big C outfit straddles the border. I own the headquarters ranch in Texas and the Santa Catalina Grant in Mexico. There's ten thousand head of cattle in Mexico and a few hundred head of good horses I want you to get out before they get slaughtered in all the shooting and pillaging that's going on here.'

Kate Crawford, better known as Cattle Kate, spilled tobacco into a brown cigarette paper, rolled it deftly with one hand and snapped a match across her thumbnail. She held the match flame cupped in her hand to light the cigarette, the yellow glow revealing for a brief moment the lines, etched by tragedy and suffering, at the corners of her mouth and eyes. There was a dangerous look in the opaque black of her eyes as she blew the flame out with the smoke.

'Write your own ticket, Bass. Salary or straight commission, or both. I'll make it worth your while to quit running guns and bootlegging.' Her white teeth flashed in a smile that reached her eyes. 'It's legitimate. The cattle are mine. But don't get the idea I'm trying to make an honest man out of you, Bass,' she said, quickly.

'It's a deal, lady.' The grin on Bass' face made him look younger.

'My friends call me Kate. I want you for a friend, Bass. We'll talk money as we ride along. It's time you got out of Hidalgo. Vamanos!'

'There's one of Villa's generals inside, in white linen store clothes.' Bass jerked a thumb toward the cantina. 'He's got money to buy the guns we just hijacked from Lobo Jones. I'll make it a quick dicker.'

Bass looked around to see General Guzman

standing in the doorway. 'That's him,' he told Kate Crawford, motioning toward Guzman.

Kate Crawford's voice was low-pitched, venomous. 'General Guzman and his hired killers.' Her hand gripped Bass' arm like a steel clamp.

'No.' Her voice was almost inaudible. 'Madre de Dios, no.' She pulled him back into the darkness and around the corner of the building, out of sight of the heavy-set Mexican with the searching eyes.

Bass felt her trembling. He put his arm around her, holding her until the trembling stopped. His other hand held a six-shooter.

'I'm all right now, Bass.' She pushed away slowly. 'I'll buy the guns.' She forced a smile as she stepped back.

'To hell with the guns,' Bass said.

'You're a good man, Bass.' She took his hand, and they went into the pitch darkness to where he had left his horse. Another saddled horse stood there, bridle reins dropped, ground tied, alongside his. They mounted and rode away in silence.

'I followed you to town, Bass,' she told him as they rode along together, the lights of the town behind them. 'It's the end of a year's trail.'

'No sabe.' Bass grinned faintly. 'I don't understand why—?'

'You'd be surprised, Bass,' she said, shifting her weight to one stirrup, twisting sideways to look at him from under the brim of her old Stetson, 'at how much I know about you, and my reasons for tracking you down and talking you into helping me out of a tight spot. Mostly they're selfish reasons. I'm not trying to be mysterious about it. It's just too long a story to tell you now. It'll have to wait till we got to the Hacienda de Santa Catalina.'

'I can wait,' Bass told her, wondering just how much she knew about him. 'I've heard a lot about you too, ma'am, but I never thought I'd be working for Cattle Kate, Dona Catalina of the Santa Catalina Grant.' He grinned faintly.

'Don't believe all you hear, Bass,' she said, her voice edged with bitterness. 'Cattle Kate had built up quite a rep for herself.' Her black eyes met his. 'You're working with me, not for me. I told you to write your own ticket.'

'A man don't take pay for helpin' a lady. That goes for the fellers that ride with me. We're proud to be of any help.'

As they rode into a bushy arroyo, Bass took the lead. He rode standing in his stirrups, his eyes searching the darkness ahead, his saddle gun in the crook of his arm.

'Who goes?' A voice barked from the brush ahead.

Bass pulled up. 'Who were you expectin'?' Bass called back. 'Go easy on the cussin'. I got a lady with me.'

'Lady?' The voice chuckled. 'Then it's time

somebody told the lady who she's been ridin' with.'

'The lady is Kate Crawford. She knows who she's ridin' with. Step out and tip your hats.'

The men rode out from the brush, pulling off their hats as Bass called them by their first names.

'Better slip the gun packs off the mules, fellers.' Bass told them. 'Turn 'em loose an' bust every gun. We're outa the gun-runnin' business. We're gatherin' cattle on the Santa Catalina range for the lady.'

'My crew need guns at the Hacienda, Bass. I have the money to buy what guns you have.'

'You got the guns, lady.' One of Bass' cowhands spoke up. 'But your money's wooden around this outfit. We're workin' for Cattle Kate, and we'll head the pack mules yonderly.'

Bass grinned at Kate Crawford as they rode in the lead of the pack train. Voices carried in the night, and they could hear the tough cowhands talking as they got pack mules strung out. It was rough talk, sprinkled with cuss words. They were cowhands, going on a big roundup, going back to the hard work that was their life.

Kate Crawford's dark eyes were misted as she reached out and took Bass' hand. 'Grin all you want, Bass.' Her voice husky. 'You'll never know what this means to me, you and your men are going into danger. I have no right to let you run the big risk you'll take when you trail that big herd of mine out of Mexico. I've changed my mind about getting my cattle out. It's not worth the risk, Bass. Let them butcher the cattle. We'll have a big barbecue and a last fiesta at the Hacienda. That ends it.'

Her hand felt cold in Bass' grip. He shook his head. 'I can't go back to Texas,' Bass said quietly. 'Every man in my outfit is in the same fix. Trailing your cattle out is no more dangerous than what we've been doing. Their hearts and minds are set on that cattle drive. Nothing can stop us now.' He gripped her hand and let go. 'But Mexico is no place for you now, Kate.'

'I'm staying,' she said. 'I was born at the Hacienda. The Santa Catalina Grant is mine. The people there were born on this land, and their families for generations have lived there. It's my place to stay with them. That's why I wanted those guns you hijacked from Lobo Jones. We'll use it on anyone who tries to drive 'em off.'

They were coming into a wide valley now, and a few minutes later they reined up at a wayside shrine. It was no more than a pile of rocks. A crudely carved, wooden image of Our Lady of Guadalupe, Patron Saint of Mexico, was set inside the rocks, underneath which a stub of candle in a broken bottle burned.

Kate made the sign of the cross. Her head was bowed, and her lips moved in prayer. A moment later her hand pointed to half a dozen crosses scattered in the mesquite bush. Then she rode around the shrine of boulders and leaned down to point to some insignia chisled into a large rock a few feet from the shrine.

Bass made the insignia out. It was the Iron Cross of Germany.

'Aleman.' The woman spoke, her voice harsh, brittle. 'El Sanguinario, The Butcher. General Kurt Guzman and his Alemanes. They rode up on a small Mexican family who had stopped to offer a prayer at the shrine. Butcher Guzman destroyed the shrine and killed the entire family. Shot them with his Luger pistol and left the bodies for the buzzards. That Iron Cross insignia was red with their blood when I rode up with my vaqueros next morning. We buried the dead, set out the crosses to mark the graves and rebuilt the shrine.

'We are on the Santa Catalina Grant now,' Kate told Bass. 'We've ben traveling on my range for the past hour. General Guzman is the Jefe, and he issued orders to tear down all shrines, destroy every cross and grave-marker. Anybody, even a child, found lighting a votive candle will be shot down.'

Her eyes were dark-shadowed as she stared into the distance, toward the mountain range that cradled the fertile valley. 'Somebody rides down the hills to keep the votive candle lit. They risk their lives every time they come.'

She crossed herself and rode on. She was choked with emotion and rode for a time in silence.

'Pancho Villa promised General Guzman the Santa Catalina Grant,' she said, her voice bitter now and her black eyes shining. 'Guzman sent me word six months ago to move out and leave everything I owned behind. I sent his messenger back with my answer—that Catalina de la Guerra Crawford would die fighting for her own. I sent word to Butcher Guzman and his Alemanes that they would be 'dobe-walled if they ever set foot on my land.'

Her lips twisted in a mirthless smile as she looked at Bass. 'Now you see the odds you are up against, Bass, if you try to get my stock out. I have tried three times. Guzman's Alemanes killed my vaqueros, stole the horses, shot down my cattle and left the dead bodies of my men to rot with the cattle his men had slaughtered wantonly. Guzman's hired killers and Lobo Jones' wolf pack of followers are the scum and filth of the border-jumper renegades. Now Guzman is recruiting mercenaries.'

She rolled and lit a cigarette. 'I need guns, guns and ammunition.' She gestured back at the pack train. 'That's all. The rest of it was a woman's foolish dream. Forget it, Bass.'

Bass thumbed his hat back, and a strange light came into his puckered gray eyes, a reckless glint that held a sparkle under the hardness. 'You're stuck with a Texan, Kate, Bass Slocum, and a hand-picked bunch of men who'll follow me through hell and high water. I got my own axe to grind down here, a double-bitted axe, and you've whetted it sharp.'

CHAPTER TWO

The Texans and Kate were riding through a bunch of cattle. Kate pointed to several steers with her Big C brand barred out, vented. A fresh Iron Cross brand that covered the whole side of a critter's hide was commencing to scab over. 'Guzman's Aleman brand,' she said.

Bass nodded grimly, sizing the cattle up. They showed signs of being chouced around and driven hard.

Kate Crawford's arm swept in a panoramic gesture that took in the whole valley ahead. 'The Hacienda de Santa Catalina,' she said softly.

It was a small Mexican village with one rambling, white-washed adobe house in the center, a scattering of small adobe huts, each with its own farm surrounding it, high mesquite corrals, close built like stockades. There were giant cottonwood and sycamore trees along both banks of a small river. As Bass looked at it in admiration, the sound of an old Spanish bell drifted to them.

'The Mission of Santa Catalina,' she explained. 'That's the alarm bell ringing now. They've sighted us.' She lifted her palomino horse to a long trot.

Kate Crawford had told Bass about the palomino stallion, the gift of Presidente Porfirio Diaz to the Santa Catalina Grant, direct strain of the Golden Horses sent from Spain as a gift to Diaz.

Bass' own quarter horse gelding, he figured, was as good, if not better, than the famous palomino strain, but he kept his opinion to himself.

Nobody was in sight when they rode up. No man, woman or child showed. The only sign of life was the barking of some dogs. As they sat their horses, the huge patio gate of the high adobe wall around the whitewashed casa swung open slowly. A girl stood there in the opening. She was wearing faded levi overalls, boots and a gray-flannel blouse. She wore no hat, and the sunrise reflected the highlights of her red hair.

She was the red-haired cantina girl Bass had called Gringita, the girl on whose account he had killed a man more than a year ago. She stood there, tall, slim, her clear amber eyes showing no recognition.

'Who's the stranger with you, Mama?' she asked, her voice sharp with suspicion.

'My daughter, Catalina Crawford.' Kate spoke to Bass in a low tone. 'You killed a drunken gringo who tried to paw at her at Laredo. Kit doesn't recognize you behind that mustache.'

The heavy gate swung wider to reveal a dozen or more armed vaqueros. A tall, slim Mexican in shabby leather charro clothes was in command. He had a six-shooter in his hand, and the gun was pointed at Bass.

'You've met before, Kit,' Kate Crawford told her daughter, and called to Pablo to put away his gun.

Recognition came into the girl's eyes. 'Tejano!' It was an odd sound that came from her parted lips, like laughter throttled by a sob.

'Gringita!' Bass said huskily as he swung from his saddle, to stand within reach of her. This girl had been in Bass' dreams for too long. He forgot that anybody was there to watch as he pulled her closer, and their lips met hungrily. It was as if the two were alone in the world.

Kate Crawford jumped her horse between the tall Mexican and the couple locked in a lover's embrace as a gun exploded in Bass' ears. He whirled, swinging the girl behind him with a swift motion that sent her reeling, off balance.

The tall Mexican had a knife in his hand now. His gun lay on the ground where Kate Crawford had knocked it from his hand. He came at Bass with a blind rush, the knife raised. Bass had a split-second look at his face that was contorted with hate.

Bass twisted sideways as the knife ripped the shoulder of his denim brush jacket. He pivoted and swung, his weight behind the fist that caught the Maxican under his lean jaw, making a spatting sound as the blow landed. The force of it lifted the man, then dropped him at Bass' feet.

Bass felt the pain shoot up into his arm from the broken knuckles of his left hand. He was breathing hard as he looked down at the fallen man's face. He was out, cold.

Bass' gun was in his hand as he looked at the other Mexicans who stood watching him, their guns in their hands.

Kate Crawford's voice was sharp, commanding as she barked orders for her vaqueros to lower the carbines they had pointed at Bass.

The pack train had come up with Bass' tough Texan cowhands. They rode into the patio, their guns ready to shoot.

Kate Crawford and her daughter Kit stood side by side, both pale.

'I hadn't counted on this, Bass.' Kate Crawford sounded worried. 'I'm sorry.'

'Poor Pablo.' Kit took a step toward the Mexican. Her mother's hand on her arm held her back.

Bass suddenly remembered that he had seen the handsome, tall Mexican before, a year or more ago at the baile in the Mexican section of Laredo. To the best of Bass' liquor-fogged recollection, this same Pablo had been jealous because Bass had taken the red-haired girl away from him. This, therefore, was not the first run-in Bass had had with the handsome Pablo.

'Pablo is the Majordomo of the Santa Catalina Grant,' Kate Crawford explained, 'as was his father and his grandfather before him. Both those men died defending the Santa Catalina and for the honor of the de la Guerras. Pablo has the blood of those men in his veins.' She spoke in the language of Mexico.

Here on the Santa Catalina, she was Dona Catalina. It was only north of the border that the woman was known as Cattle Kate of the Big C outfit that had belonged to her Texan husband, Will Crawford. Hers was a delicate situation, requiring all her diplomacy, and with it all the understanding and help Bass could give her. In Mexico hatred for the gringo Texan ran strong.

Bass slid his six-shooter back into its holster. Pablo was moving. A groan came from behind his clenched teeth as he sat up. Hate filled his black eyes as Bass bent over to help him to his feet. He slapped Bass' helping hand aside.

'Keep your gringo hands off me!' Pablo spat at him.

Bass licked the blood off his skinned knuckles that had commenced to swell. 'Have it your own way,' he said.

As Bass took a step back, the high heel of his boot trampled on the six-inch blade of thin steel. It made a metallic sound as the blade broke off near the hilt. Pablo walked over to where his six-shooter lay and picked it up. Bass had his hand on his gun as he watched Pablo, gun in hand, hesitate for a long moment. The eyes of the two men met and held across the short distance, gripped in deadly enmity that could have only one outlet, but this was neither the time nor the place.

Then the young Major Domo barked staccato orders to his vaqueros. He tried to put a swagger in his step as he went through the gateway, his men following. Bass' Texans reined aside to watch the vaqueros file past.

'The pack mules,' one of Bass' Texans said with a careless indifference, 'would sure like to get shed of their packs. Where would you want the guns left, ma'am?'

'Tell my Major Domo to get fresh mules to take the guns. Pablo knows as good a place as any to put them,' Kate Crawford said. 'Every gun and box of ammunition will have to be hidden until my Mexicans can come in from the hills. It's against the law for my vaqueros to carry firearms. They hide their guns whenever the Federal soldiers come here on their weekly patrol.' She spoke with bitterness.

'You boys,' Bass called to his men. 'You'd better slip those packs and turn the mules loose. I look for that Federalista patrol to ride up before long. They been skylinin' this outfit since daybreak. I'll be over at the stockade directly. Take care of my horse, and throw my saddle on a fresh one and saddle fresh horses yourselves.'

They rode off, pulling the heavy gate closed behind them. Bass and the two women were left alone now.

'It's all my fault,' Kit said. 'I acted like a silly darn fool.'

'You come by it natural, Kit.' Her mother put an arm across the girl's shoulders as she spoke to Bass. 'Pablo takes his Major Domo job seriously, and Pablo has been in love with Kit since I brought her here in pigtails.'

Kate spoke now to her daughter. 'It was your mother, Kit, who brought Bass and his men and the guns here, more or less under false pretenses.'

'No, ma'am.' Bass shook his head. 'We came of our own free will.'

'One reason I brought you here, Bass,' Kate said, 'was to keep this headstrong daughter of mine from running off to track you down. I thought it was only her guilty conscience that was bothering her when she disappeared, leaving you to take the blame for killing a man. She'd have stayed, but Pablo got her away that night. Kit has worried and fretted about it for over a year, and I've shared her worry. When I found you, Bass, I brought you to her. I had to find out if what she said was true—that she was in love with you.' She took Bass' hand and put her daughter's hand in his.

'I broke every rule and tradition of the de la Guerras when I ran off with a Texan named Will Crawford,' Kate said. A smile softened the hard-bitten lines around her mouth. 'Will Crawford's outfit was across the Rio Grande that marked the north boundary of the Santa Catalina Grant. Our brand was a Big C, and Will had that same Big C registered as his in the Texas brand book. Will Crawford was a cattle rustler. He built his herd up from the wet cattle he stole from the Santa Catalina Grant. There was a price on his head in Mexico when I met him on one of his pasears across the border.' Her eyes were shining now with the memory of it.

'It was early morning, and I was alone,' she said. 'I was riding out a two-year-old palomino stud, given to me on my seventeenth birthday, when this red-headed Texan rode up. He said his name was Will Crawford, and that he had crossed the border to steal one of the Santa Catalina Golden Horses, a young stallion he wanted for a remuda stud.'

Kate's eyes softened at the memory as she went on. 'He pointed to the horse I was riding, and a grin spread across his freckled, homely face. "Never let it be said," he told me, taking off his hat and bowing stiffly, "that a Texan ever set a lady afoot. If you will ride across the river to my ranch, I will give you the pick of my remuda."'

Kate laughed softly. 'So I went along. The Texas Rangers picked us up at Palofox on the Texas side of the Rio Grande. The charges against Will Crawford were horsestealing and kidnapping. One thing, and only one thing on earth, could save the Texan's life, the Ranger Captain told us both. There was no law on either side of the border could lay a hand on Will Crawford if I was to marry the man of my own free will, without threat or coercion.

'I lied twice that day at Palofox—about my age, and when I said I had crossed the border willingly to become the wife of Will Crawford.'

A hard glint crept into the woman's eyes. 'Captain Clay McCoy, a young church deacon, said he would marry us on one condition—that Will Crawford takes an oath never to cross the border again, and never to steal any horses or cattle from the Santa Catalina Grant. Will took the oath. His life was at stake that Sunday morning. Both the Ranger Captain and I were aware of it. It was only the redheaded Will Crawford who seemed indifferent to the whole thing. He never once by word or action tried to beg out of it. He had a grin on his homely freckled face and a look of mockery in his green eyes when he took the oath and the vows of marriage.'

Kate Crawford's arm tightened around the shoulders of Kit. 'It was only when Will was shot down a few years afterward that I knew he had violated his sworn oath not to steal. It was not in the nature of Will Crawford to be bound in any way by the laws of man.'

Her voice trailed off, her eyes dark with bitter memories. Then she picked up the broken continuity of her story. 'My father never relented. The price on the red head of Will Crawford was doubled after we were married. After Will was dead and my father was dying, he sent for me. He had been wounded in a gun fight with bandits who were rustling his cattle. Two of my brothers were killed, along with Pablo's father, who was Major Domo at the time. I was the last of the de la Guerras. If I refused the responsibilities that entailed the heritage of the Santa Catalina Grant, the title would revert to the Republic of Mexico, my father told me. I accepted those responsibilities when I became sole owner. I owed that much to Don Carlos, my father, and to the families who have lived on the Grant for generations.

'Now,' Kate said, 'Guzman's Alemanes have driven most of those families back into the hills. This Hacienda is deserted now. The men come down at night from the hills to tend their crops as best they can. Only Pablo and his handful of men remain to guard us. There are about a hundred able-bodied men who are fit to make a hard ride and fight, but they have no guns or cartridges. The Federalistas, fearing my men would join the Villistas, have confiscated all the guns they could find.'

Dona Catalina faced Bass and her daughter. 'I have managed to procure a blanket visa for them and their families to cross into Texas. That's the business that took me to Hidalgo. I'd just crossed the river from Palofox, where Captain Clay McCoy signed the paper.

'My Major Domo will send word into the hills for the head of each family to come here. I will put it up to those men, and they will decide whether they want to cross the border into Texas to my headquarters ranch, or stay here to be shot down by Guzman's Alemanes or the mercenaries he is hiring.'

The woman's dark eyes looked out across the high wall of the patio into the distant hills, where the Mexican families had fled. There they were prey for the warlike Yaquis. Nor were they safe from the Federal cavalry who prowled the hills, shooting down every man as a rebel suspect, pillaging and raping as they rode their ruthless way.

The customary rules of war did not govern either faction. The Federalistas, or the Alemanes, who were said to be in alliance with the Villistas, were blood-spattered with the same guilt.

Bass listened in silence while the woman had laid bare the things she had kept locked up for too long inside her. Even her own daughter had never known what her mother had just related. All that Bass had ever heard concerning the legendary Kate Crawford was true. The tragedy of her life had been barely sketched in the telling of it. He could fill in the rest. The splendid courage of the woman, the heartaches, the bitter disappointments, the unshed tears of the years that had left etched lines on her leathery skin.

Bass was trying to find the right words to tell her that he and his Texans were at her command when the old Spanish bell started ringing. The heavy gates swung open, and Bass' Texans sat their horses on the outside.

One of them rode up to him and said, 'Looks like we got company comin', Bass.' The man spoke carelessly. 'I brought your horse.'

'Federalistas, or Butcher Guzman's Alemanes?' asked Bass.

'Too far away to tell.' The Texan lit a half-smoked cigarette that hung from a corner of his mouth. 'About twenty-five horsebackers, for a range count. They shouldn't give us too much trouble.'

'Has my Major Domo gone?' asked Kate Crawford.

'Yes ma'am.' He cocked his head up at the belfry of the old mission. 'Does that bell ring by itself, lady?' he asked.

'There's an old Mexican, swinging at the end of the bell rope. If my Major Domo hears the alarm, he'll turn back.' Dona Catalina looked at Bass. 'How many guns were in those packs, Bass?' she asked.

'About one hundred 30-30 Winchester carbines. Probably a hundred rounds of ammunition for each gun.'

'Then there will be a hundred of my vaqueros with the Major Domo when he shows up. Pablo's itching for trouble.'

Bass was watching the distant riders as they fanned out down the long hill, about a mile distant. The faint note of a bugle sounded as the bell stopped ringing.

'That's a detachment of Federalista Cavalry,' Bass said. 'Lobo Jones and his wolf pack don't travel in cavalry formation, and it's too far from their town barracks for Butcher Guzman's Alemanes to travel.' Bass looked at both women. 'Unless your Major Domo and his vaqueros get here inside half an hour, the gun ruckus will be over. If you ladies will step inside the house and lock the doors, I'll close the gate as I go out.'

The woman's hand was on Bass' arm. The bleak look in her eyes held him. 'I can't afford trouble with the Federalistas, Bass. That's Captain Vidal on his inspection patrol. He's arrogant and vain. I've handled him before. I can handle him again.' Her eyes had a stricken look. 'Until I get those Mexican families across the border, I have to get along with the Federalistas, who are still in power.

'If you and your Texans could hide out, Bass,' she continued, 'I'd like to settle this without gun trouble or bloodshed. Let me give it a try. You can hide out in the stockade. I'll call out if I need help. There's too much at stake right now to stir up further trouble, the lives of women and children back in the hills. I wish you'd let me handle Captain Vidal and his soldiers.'

'Whatever you say, Kate.' Bass gave in, but with reluctance. 'We'll be in the stockade. Leave the gate open.'

Kit moved quickly as Bass was about to mount. Her arms went around his neck, and her mouth bruised his. Then she pushed him away, her amber eyes shining.

Bass swung into the saddle and rode with his men into the high mesquite stockade. When the heavy gate swung shut, one of his tough Texans chuckled softly. 'I've heard tell,' came the lazy drawl, 'that a feller in love can go for days without grub, like a camel without water.'

'Yeah,' spoke another Texan. 'Nothin' like one of them Mexican barbecues to take the wrinkles out of a man's belly.'

'I look for this Don Bassito to shore throw a big fiesta, wine, women and guitar music. I got my heart set on that,' said another man.

'Viva Don Bassito!' they chorused.

'Hush your big mouths!' Bass warned them. 'Here come the soldiers!'

'Get a look at the purty feller workin' in the lead of that ragged-assed 'dobe outfit,' one man chuckled. 'Don Bassito had better hightail it back to ride close herd on his best gal. I wouldn't trust grandmaw around that high-chinned purty bastard.'

The bugle sounded as the horsemen came into sight, riding four abreast. Some were beardless youths, others older, seasoned soldiers. They were all dust-grimed in dirty, wrinkled uniforms, with cartridge belts sagging their shoulders. They were armed with pistols and machetes, their carbines in grimy hands. Their horses were marked by dried sweat and were leg-weary. The men were all stamped with the same sullen look, the older men especially marked with the brutality of their calling. They had all shot down men lined in front of an adobe wall.

El Capitan Vidal's yellow boots were freshly polished, his tailored whipcord breeches and blouse brushed. His lantern jaw was clean-shaven, his trim mustache twisted, the ends waxed. He sat his cavalry saddle with a stiff-backed arrogance, his black eyes darting swift looks around, then focusing on the opened gates that led into the large, tiled patio, where Dona Catalina stood alone.

She had changed her cowhand garb for a plain black dress. A black mantilla covered her cropped gray hair. She looked like she belonged in this setting. There was something about this tall, handsome woman in black that demanded respect.

Captain Vidal raised a gloved hand, and a

sergeant barked his order to halt. Captain Vidal saluted stiffly before he spoke. 'At sunrise this morning, a pack train of twenty-five mules, loaded with contraband guns and ammunition, arrived here. I saw the mules in your pasture. An hour ago the contraband was packed on fresh mules and taken into the hills, presumably by the gringo gun-runners in charge of the pack train. It is my unpleasant duty to place you under arrest, Senora Crawford. It will be my painful duty to have you shot by a firing squad for this crime.' The Federalista Captain spoke in the same staccato voice he used on the parade ground. He twisted the waxed ends of his little mustache as he sat stiff-backed in his saddle.

'You are indeed a brave man, El Capitan Vidal. A very brave soldier.' Dona Catalina's voice was brittle, like breaking glass. 'You combine strategy with your splendid courage. You timed it to arrive after the pack train and the men had gone, and you know I'd be alone. There should be a special medal for your special brand of valiant deed, El Capitan Vidal.'

The Captain's face flushed, his thin lips peeling back to show his white teeth. 'Your sarcasm is ill-timed, Senora. My courage and the bravery of my men has been proven many times. My delayed arrival here had its purpose.

'The punishment for the crime you have committed is death,' Vidal added. 'However, I shall make a compromise. Deliver the contraband to me here, and let the gringo gunrunners lay down their guns and surrender without gunfire. When that is done to my satisfaction, your life shall be spared. I give you my word of honor as an officer in the Federal Army of the Republic of Mexico!'

'I was wondering, El Capitan Vidal.' Her voice was heavy with sarcasm. 'What will become of these men if they surrender?'

'The gringos will be executed, naturally.'

'Naturally.' The woman repeated. 'And afterward, El Capitan, after those men have been shot down, what happens to me and to my daughter? To the Santa Catalina Grant that belongs to us?'

'I shall offer you armed escort across the Rio Grande so that you and your daughter can return to Texas. The Santa Catalina Grant will be confiscated by the Government of Mexico, together with all livestock.'

'What happens to the Mexican families who have lived on the Santa Catalina Grant for generations? What becomes of them?'

'The able-bodied men will be drafted into the Army of the Republic of Mexico. The older men and the women and children will be allowed to remain unmolested on their lands.'

El Capitan Vidal slapped his boot with his riding crop. 'Enough of this talk. My soldiers are hungry. They need food and something stronger than water to drink, fresh horses later. Send a messenger to carry out my orders. Your life and the safety of your daughter depend on your decision. I demand your answer without further delay.'

A door at the far side of the patio was flung open. Pablo, Major Domo of the Santa Catalina Grant, stood framed in the doorway. The silver-handled six-shooter in his hand was pointed at the lean belly of El Capitan Vidal. 'I hold the answer for the Dona Catalina in my hand!' Pablo's teeth showed in a flat grin.

Captain Vidal was reaching for his pistol when the Major Domo shot him through the head. The shot acted as a signal. Guns spewed fire from all sides. Pablo slammed the heavy gates shut as he ran out to leave the women alone in the patio.

Behind the stockade, Bass' voice sounded saw-edged. 'Let 'em fight it out.'

Bass and his Texans, peering out through the high stockade, watched the Major Domo and his vaqueros creep up on the soldiers from all sides. The vaqueros had left their horses in the brush and came up on foot, so many of them that Bass lost count. Outside the stockade was a bedlam of noise, gunfire, shouting and cursing. The screams of the wounded pierced the yells of Pablo's vaqueros. The pitched battle turned quickly into a slaughter and massacre, no mercy shown, no quarter asked.

Bass and his men waited, their guns gripped

in their hands, for the slaughter to end, for the shooting to die down.

'Pablo's my meat,' Bass told his men. 'Shoot that quick-triggered bastard, and the guts will go out of the rest of them.'

The shooting was dying down when the mission bell started clanging. The gunfire stopped as the last echoes of the bell faded.

'Pablo!' called Dona Catalina in a sharp voice. 'Tell every man to bring his gun inside the patio. You, too, Pablo. Those are orders from Dona Catalina. I want them obeyed without a word of question, without delay.'

Dona Catalina opened the gates wide. She was standing there in her black dress, erect, her head held high, her face white against the black rebozo that covered her hair, her eyes black and fathomless. There was the pride of the de la Guerras in her bearing, a fierce, high-strung pride and splendid courage.

The scattered dead lay in the heavy dust, along with a few of the horses that had been shot down. There were no wounded. Pablo's gun had attended to that as he walked among the dead. His charro pants were spattered from the blood of dead men. His hands shook a little as he ejected the empty shells from his gun and shoved fresh cartridges into the empty chambers, the gun-barrel still hot.

Pablo faced the woman in black, a mirthless grin on his lips that thinned into a snarl of defiance. Still drunk from the tequila he had swilled down and the blood he had spilled, Pablo was breathing heavily.

'I hold the gun that belonged to my dead father.' Pablo's voice was harsh. 'And my father's father. I surrender this gun to no man on earth. I defended your life and your daughter's honor with this gun. I keep my gun woman!'

'*Woman!*' She spat at him. 'I am Dona Catalina de Guerra. Show your proper respect, hombre. You take the orders I give you, or leave.'

'I surrender my gun to no man or woman.' Pablo spoke defiantly. 'If I leave, my men go with me. We have guns and cartridges. We know how to fight.'

'Go, then, Pablo. Keep your guns because you will soon have need of them.' She lifted her voice so that the others who had come up could hear. They were sweat-sodden, blood-spattered, their eyes glazed, sullen and bewildered by all the talk.

'I would not have any of you surrender your guns,' Dona Catalina told them. 'Mexico and the Santa Catalina Grant is no longer safe for you or your families. I have a blanket visa that will allow you and your families to cross the border into the United States. I have homes for you on my ranch in Texas when you cross the river. Go into the hills now and bring your families, and every horse and pack mule you can round up. Bring them in before sunrise tomorrow.

'Whether Pablo goes or stays makes little difference. When a Major Domo refuses to take orders from his Patron, he is of no further use.'

She raised her arm and pointed in the direction of the stockade. 'Inside the stockade are the Tejanos who brought the guns and cartridges you now have. When I offered them money, they refused payment. Pablo would have you shoot down these Tejanos with the very guns they have given you. Pablo puts his own jealous hatred for their leader before the loyalty he owes the Santa Catalina and its people. Let any man who is in sympathy with Pablo and is in favor of killing the Tejanos, think twice before he lifts a gun.

'Bassito and his Texans are fighting men,' she went on. 'They would slaughter you as you slaughtered these soldiers. Pablo would be killed by the first bullet. He makes an easy target right now. I have only to give Bassito a signal, shout a command, or raise an arm, and some of you who are now alive would be dead in your tracks.'

The silence that followed her words was like the hushed lull before a storm. It was an uneasy silence, charged with destruction. These men had the taste of spilled blood in their mouths. Their nostrils were clogged with the smell of powder smoke, the smell of death. Their eyes were fixed on the high stockade where Bass and his men sat their horses behind the closed gate.

'The Dona Catalina,' said one of the Texans who spoke in the Mexican tongue, 'has the deal. The lady holds aces.' His words carried across the crowd who were bunched together.

'Bet high when the lady opens the jackpot,' Bass called out.

'When do we eat?' one of the Texans wanted to know.

That last remark eased the tension. There was a shifting among the Mexicans.

'The Tejanos,' spoke Dona Catalina, 'are impatient from hunger. Those who would go with Pablo will depart without further delay. Those who are loyal will remain to bury these dead soldiers before departing for the hills to bring their families here. There is no further time to waste words.'

Pablo turned away, stepped around, or over, the dead soldiers in the dust. 'Vamanos, hombrecitos,' his sullen voice called to the dozen Mexicans who made up his hand-picked followers. No more than half a dozen followed Pablo back a quarter of a mile to the brush where they had left their horses.

When Pablo and his half-dozen men had gone, Dona Catalina spoke again to the others. She thanked them all in the name of the Senor Dios for their loyalty.

Bass leaned from his saddle to shove the heavy gate open and rode out, his men following, their carbines in the saddle scabbards, their six-shooters back in their holsters. Bass told his men to scatter out, to keep a sharp lookout for Lobo Jones and his wolf pack, for Guzman's Alemanes, and for any peon raids.

Bass dismounted and handed his bridle reins to one of his men and told him to put the horse in the stable with the palomino belonging to Dona Catalina. 'Ride in when you hear the dinner bell,' he told his men.

Bass was alone as he walked toward the open patio. He had to step around the scattered dead soldiers. He felt empty-bellied and a little sick, but he tried not to show it as he walked past the Mexicans, who all eyed him as he passed.

A large red earthenware olla, filled with drinking water, hung near the patio gate, a gourd dipper on a rawhide thong alongside it. Bass stopped and drank, then walked into the patio, his hat in his hand, over to where the woman in black was standing.

Her face had the color of old ashes, her eyes deep wells of black. Bass knew that she was traveling on her nerve now. He knew that the Mexicans outside were watching them, their ears strained to catch every spoken word. Bass stopped and bowed stiffly, remembering the formality of the Mexican customs.

'Enter your house.' Dona Catalina made a small gesture, then walked alongside him to the same door that Pablo had used to make his entrance. They entered the house and closed the door, just as Dona Catalina swayed dizzily. Bass caught her in time to break the fall. He carried her in his arms down the short hallway to a large room with heavy old Spanish furniture and tapestries. Heavy shutters were across the barred windows. Bass put the limp woman on a big couch.

Kit Crawford was nowhere in sight, and Bass was wondering what to do for the woman who had fainted, when a pounding noise came from behind a closed door.

Kit's voice sounded muffled on the other side. 'Let me out—! Open this door—! I'll smother to death in this closet! Mama! Bass—!'

Bass tried the big iron latch. 'It's locked,' he called.

'Get the key from the niche behind the statue of the Lady of Guadalupe on the mantel. I'm about to smother to death in here,' Kit told him.

The carved wooden image of the patron saint showed in the light of the votive candle in a red glass. Bass found the large key and fitted it into the keyhole of the ornate, wrought-iron scrollwork lock.

When he opened the door, Kit stumbled into his arms. Her cheeks were flushed, filmed with perspiration, her heavy, coppery hair tumbled in a thick tangle. Bass felt her tremble in his arms that held her tight. A sob rose in her throat as her red lips pressed against his mouth.

There was something untamed, savage in that kiss, the full red lips quivering against his mouth as the length of her slim body pressed against him. Her half-lidded amber eyes were fever-bright as her lips moved and clung in a wordless message.

Kit released herself from his embrace as her mother came into the room.

'I passed out, Kit,' Dona Catalina was saying. 'It was ghastly. Brutal and savage. You can be thankful I locked you in the closet to spare you the sight of that horrible butchery.' A shudder gripped the older woman, and her face was ashen-gray. 'Get some brandy, Kit. We can all use a drink. Get the women out of the cellar and put them to work. Bass and his Texans are starved.'

When Kit came back with the brandy and glasses, she reported that the women had been on their knees down in the wine cellar, praying, terrified. They wept with joy when she told them the battle was over, and that it was safe to come out.

'I offer no excuse for Pablo and his vaqueros, Bass,' Kate Crawford told Bass, her dark eyes troubled. 'This is Mexico. What happened was bound to come sooner or later.' Her slim band reached into the low neckline of her dress and withdrew a deadly little .44

Derringer pistol.

'General Guzman,' she said, 'His an ugly brute, part Aleman, part Mexican. He comes from that German colony below the border. They're all cast-out criminals, exiled from Germany, stolid, stupid brutes who work their women in the fields. General Guzman has some fantastic notion of taking Texas for himself, setting up his own kingdom, riding on the heels of Pancho Villa and his rebel army. He salutes no flag. He owes allegiance to no country.

'Lobo Jones patterns his ways after Guzman. He travels on his tough shape and takes orders from the General. The man is out in the open with his drunken toughness.

'El Capitan Vidal, on the other hand, comes from a line of brave soldiers, all of them men of honor, soldiers and politicos of high esteem, but he wants the Santa Catalina Grant for himself, and he wants Kit along with it. He lied when he promised us safe escort into Texas.

'So,' finished Kate Crawford, 'brutal and ruthless as that massacre was, I cannot feel too sorry for El Capitan Vidal and his men. Pablo and his vaqueros saved you an ugly chore, Bass.'

Bass nodded, smiling grimly. 'And what about Pablo?' he asked.

Kate Crawford filled the brandy glasses. 'Salud!' she said, and they drank.

'My Major Domo had to be disciplined,'

Kate said. 'Pablo will come back with his apologies when he has time to cool off that hot temper of his. I look for him to return by sunrise. Pablo and his men will take my orders then without argument or rebellion. They will give us armed escort to the border and across the river to my Texas headquarters ranch. There will be a large cavalcade—wagons, carts, burros, pack mules, horses, women, children, dogs and chickens.

'Thanks to you and your Texans, there'll be a hundred men armed, ready to fight off any enemy attack.'

She hesitated, her eyes shadowed with brooding thought. 'It is best that you and your men travel separately, Bass. You saw how those Mexicans eyed you when you passed. You are Tejano; gringo Tejano, and the bitterness, distress and hatred against all Texans, built up over the years, is deeper than you think. I married a Texan, and my daughter is part Texan. My father never forgave Will Crawford, and these Mexicans of the Santa Catalina Grant share that feeling of hatred. Kit and I travel on dangerous ground. If you and your Texans were to go with us—' Her hands made a helpless gesture.

Bass understood all too well. He felt the same resentment toward Pablo and his Mexicans. A flat grin spread Bass' mouth. Only the coldness of his gun-metal eyes betrayed his real feelings.

'Back yonder at Hidalgo,' Bass reminded her quietly, 'you talked about some horses and cattle you wanted out of Mexico. We'll pull out at daybreak. We'll need a remuda of good cow horses and pack mules, and flour, beans and coffee. We'll have enough cattle to throw on the trail by tomorrow evenin', and we'll build our herd as we go along. We'll be trompin' your heels when you cross the Rio Grande, and you'd better have your Major Domo and his Mexicans on the Texas side of the border to receive 'em. Bass Slocum and his Texans turn back at the river.'

Bass poured his glass full of brandy and tossed it off. 'I better get out with my gringo Texans where I belong,' he called back from the threshold as the door closed behind him.

Bass was in an ugly frame of mind as he crossed the patio, his spur rowels jangling with each step. Perhaps it was the potent brandy splashed in on an empty belly, but Bass had the notion that he and his men had been used.

Kate Crawford stood at the barred window, the heavy drapes held back, and watched Bass cross the patio, his hat slanted across his eyes, his right hand brushing the butt of his holstered gun.

'Damn!' Her hands were clenched.

'Bass will get over it.' Kit stood alongside her mother. 'Before morning.'

'I know, Kit. I was thinking about something else. The tomorrow beyond that, when he turns back at the Rio Grande, because he killed a drunken spur jingler who held a commission in the Texas Rangers. Bass is outlawed in Texas, Kit.'

'Then I'll stay here in Mexico with him.'

Her mother shook her head. 'Bass is a bandit in Mexico and an outlaw in Texas. A woman has no place in the life of a man like that. He knows it, and I know it. He's blaming me now for bringing him here. I'm blaming myself. I needed those guns, and I needed Bass and his Texans. I lied to him, tricked him with a woman's underhanded treachery.'

'Stop it, Mama!' Kit cut in. 'You're the finest, bravest, most unselfish person on earth. Bass understands. If he doesn't, he will before tonight is over.'

The eyes of mother and daughter met and held. Then they were in each other's arms. Holding Kit in an almost animal protective embrace, the mother voiced a silent prayer. 'Let the Senor Dios be merciful to you, child. May He guide and protect you in your love for this man.'

CHAPTER THREE

The Mexican vaqueros were busy taking what they needed from the bodies of the dead soldiers as Bass walked out. Cartridge belts and ammunition, guns, machetes, army shoes, if they were in good condition, prize booty. The vaqueros were sullen, unfriendly, and Bass eyed them with cold wariness, his right hand brushing his holstered gun with each step he took.

One man was bent over the dead body of El Capitan Vidal. He was pulling the polished yellow cavalry boot off. He gave a hard jerk, the boot came off, the dead foot thudding into the heavy dust. He removed the other boot, also the cartridge belt and Luger pistol. He held the pistol palmed in his hand as he looked at Bass.

The vaquero was a rawboned man, nearly seven feet tall, darker skinned than the others. Deep lines were etched on his lean-jawed, flat-planed, beardless face and around the corners of his thin-lipped mouth. The man's face was more Indian than Mexican. He stood there, his big felt sombrero at an angle across his sharp eyes. He wore a faded, blood-spattered cotton shirt and faded blue denim jeans that fit tightly around his long, saddle-warped legs that were spread a little to plant his bare feet in thong cowhide sandals, in the blood-puddled dirt. Bass sensed in him a sternness to be reckoned with on this man's own terms.

'You sabe the working of this pistola, Tejano?' He spoke in the flat, harsh voice of one given little to talking, as if the words were forced out from a voice box grown rusty and hard-caked from days and weeks of silence. His huge, bony, sinewy hand shoved the Luger, butt first, at Bass.

Bass nodded as he took hold of the well-oiled, well-kept automatic.

The German-made Luger was the finest gun of its kind, a handsome, beautiful, precision-made weapon, well-balanced and deadly in its accuracy, but requiring the care given any automatic hand gun to keep the mechanism free from dirt.

There was a smear of fresh blood on the whitewashed adobe wall of the patio, where some Mexican had wiped his hand. The distance was fifty, sixty feet. Bass balanced the Luger in his hand for a moment; the gun no higher than the level of his own sagging cartridge belt. He thumbed the safety free and aimed at the target. The Luger stuttered in the grip of his hand, spitting a stream of split-second flame, the steel-jacket bullets spattering into the thick adobe. The red smear was no longer here, only the pocks made by the eight bullets embedded there, that the palm of a woman's hand could cover.

Bass pressed the button that released the empty clip, handing the clip and the smoking gun to the vaquero. He turned his back on the man and walked away, his belly muscles tight, a cold chill wiring along his spine.

Bass had a notion he had called the giant's hand, whatever the man had had in mind, but a man could not gamble too much on it or on anything for that matter, below the border among the gringo-hating Mexcans. The odds were worse than even whether or not a bullet would break his spine.

The cold sweat had not dried when Bass reached the barn. His belly was still tight when he rode out to where his Texans sat their horses.

'You figger that got you anything?' asked one of them, his grin leaving his eyes cold. 'Of all the damn fool tricks! Takin' the guy's gun away to show off some fancy target practice.'

The big mission bell started ringing. Bass reined his horse around and started back at a high lope, without any explanation for the target practice. He called back to his men, 'Come and get the grub, you starved-to-death sons!'

Dona Catalina and her daughter stood under the thatched roof of the huge ramada, near the long table, loaded with all manner of Mexican food. There were stacks of tortillas, frijoles, chili con carne, tamales, enchiladas, tacos, and large platters of beef from the barbecue pits that held three whole steers. Big earthenware ollas, filled with sour red wine, hung from the roof, and jugs of tequila were at one end of the table.

Bass told his men to tie into the food while he walked over to speak to Dona Catalina and to Kit, who now wore a gay fiesta dress. 'I acted like a damn fool, going off like I did, Kate.' Bass grinned, shamefaced.

'Forget it, Bass. I made it sound like I was cutting you into the culls. Kit and I don't stand any too good, right now. Remember I married a Tejano. They have never forgiven me for that, and they never will.' Kate nodded toward the vaquero who had Captain Vidal's cartridge belt and Luger gun strapped on. 'Yaqui is the only one of them I can trust to the limit.'

'Yaqui?'

'You showed him how to use a Luger,' Dona Catalina smiled. 'He has no other name. He's a Yaqui Indian. Pablo's father was Major Domo when he found Yaqui, who was about fifteen at the time, riding one of our palominos. They were going to 'dobe-wall the boy. I was a little girl then, and when I cried and made a scene, my father, Don Carlos, sent the firing squad away.

'When my father tried to send Yaqui to his people, the boy refused to leave. He spoke no more than a few words of Mexican, but he made it understood that his life belonged to the little girl who had saved him from the firing squad. And because a true Yaqui would rather die by his own hand than surrender, he could never go back to his own people with the mark of disgrace branded on him. The Majordomo had branded the Santa Catalina Big C on the boy's chest.

'So Yaqui stayed. He slept outside my

window at night, followed me wherever I went to protect me. Not even my own father dared lay a hand on me. Yaqui grew to be the most feared man on the Santa Catalina Grant.

'When I married Will Crawford and lived on the Texas ranch, Yaqui went with me. When I camp back with Kit, Yaqui came with us, and his loyalty and devotion takes in Kit as well as myself.

'Pablo's heritage gave him the position of Major Domo here, but it is Yaqui who is actually in charge of everything. The vaqueros laugh—behind Pablo's back, mocking his strutting and boasting, but nobody laughs at Yaqui. There is nothing there to laugh at.' She made a motion, and Yaqui approached.

His faded pants were shoved into the tops of the boots that were losing something of their polish. The boots had been too small for his large, splayed feet. He had remedied that by cutting away the heels and soles and lacing the uppers to bullhide soles of his discarded huaraches. He had discarded the military spurs, buckling on a pair of handmade Mexican spurs with rowels as big as saucers.

'The Senor Bass and his Tejanos,' she told Yaqui, 'are driving as many cattle as they can handle to the Texas headquarters ranch. They will use the pack mules that fetched the guns, but they will need good horses. Ten horses to each string. See to it that the horses are shod, and the mules, too.' She smiled faintly. 'Tell

Senor Bass where he can locate the cattle, Yaqui.'

'El Lobo,' Yaqui spoke in his harsh, unused tone of voice, 'and his men are holding more than six thousand head of cattle in the upper valley of the Santa Catalina, the land claimed by the Alemanes. The cattle are the finest and best of our herd. The desechos have been cut back and the herd trimmed and ready to go on the trail. All are in good shape and on good feed. The Alemanes have been building big corrals and branding chutes. The Big C brand will be barred out, and the stolen cattle put into the iron cross brand of the Alemanes. El Lobo and his gringo wolf pack will trail them to Juarez and across the Rio Grande to the El Paso stockyards.'

Yaqui looked into Bass' hard, gray eyes, then went on. 'El Lobo has left twenty of his gringos there to ride herd on the cattle. There will be more Alemanes camped at the corrals, but they are agrarians, farmers, who will be on foot. They're foot soldiers who have guns and have been trained to march, goose-step, with the Alemanes.' A faint grin of contempt flattened Yaqui's mouth.

Bass lit the cigarette he had rolled. 'Six thousand head is a lot of cattle, Yaqui,' Bass said. 'We might have to whittle off what we can handle in a quick drive and come back for the rest.'

Yaqui's teeth showed in what was meant for

a grin. It made Bass shiver inside.

' 'Sta bueno.' Yaqui took the Luger from its holster, then a filled clip from the cartridge belt that sagged across his lean flank and held them toward Bass. 'The pistola,' he said. 'I no sabe the loading of it.'

Bass showed him how to slide the first cartridge into the breech, how to thumb the safety catch into place, and told him about keeping it oiled and cleaned.

Yaqui slid the Luger into its holster. 'The pistola is of Aleman make.' His eyes glittered. 'I shall use it to shoot General Guzman between the eyes, like you shoot at the mark in the adobe wall, Senor Bass Tejano.' He turned to Dona Catalina. 'I'll go now to select the horses, the finest in all Mexico.' With that he stalked off.

* * *

The sun had gone down. The Mexican families were coming in from the hills, and the place was overrun with women and children. They flocked around the long table where the food was still piled high, and a strange excitement swept over them. Dona Catalina and Kit moved through the group, stopping to talk to each family.

Candles burned inside the old mission. The doors were open, and the church was filled with kneeling, praying, black-shawled women.

Bass had shaven and washed up. Kit sought him out in the purple dusk. She took his hand and led him toward the old mission doorway.

'You are not of our faith, Bass,' she said softly, 'and I have no wish to thrust it upon you, but my mother is inside, praying. Is it too much to ask of you to go in and kneel beside her?'

Bass shook his head and kissed her gently, Kit put a black Spanish shawl, embroidered with red roses, over her head.

They went in and knelt on either side of Dona Catalina. Bass, who had renounced God, felt strangely awed in the dim candlelight. After awhile Kit and Bass left, leaving her mother there. Without a word, Kit led the way into the darkened house. She closed the door softly, turning the key in the lock.

They stood there, close together, for a long moment, in the heavy darkness. Then her arms went around his neck, and her lips found his mouth. He picked her up in his arms and groped his way into the open doorway of the nearest room. It was the one into which he had carried Kit's mother a few hours ago.

Bass' heart pounded the blood into his throat and temples. He felt dizzy, weak-kneed, as if the drinks he had consumed during the day had caught up with him. He felt his knees touch the edge of a big, old divan against the whitewashed adobe wall. The girl's mouth was against his, her soft lips clinging, as if she was saying something there in the darkness, while her arms tightened about him and her fingers moved in his hair.

Bass felt her shivering through the thin cotton of her gay-colored fiesta dress, as if she was chilled. Yet, the feverish warmth of her body came through the dress into his hands. She twisted suddenly, still clinging to him, and the sudden movement caught him off-balance, so that they fell forward together and lay there, breathless, on the divan.

Bass knew that Kit was frightened now, her shy boldness gone. Her arms relaxed, and he caressed her gently. After a time the tenseness gradually left her. They were quiet together in the dark for a time without movement, Bass' hands feeling the soft, silky texture of her hair that lay tumbled on the pillow. He dared not move for fear of frightening her back into that shivering tenseness.

Bass could make out her slim contours, the oval of her white face against the coppery, tumbled hair. He felt her eyes watching him, looking at his face to read what was there. The girl was like a colt that had never known a man's touch. One wrong move, and Bass knew that she would be gone.

He had held her close and kissed her that night at the baile at Laredo, and her lips had been warm and yielding, like they had been tonight. It was as if she was eager to give her love, but now something was holding her back.

She wanted him as he wanted her. She had led him into the church, and they had knelt there beside her mother. There was no padre to say the words that would make them man and wife, but Bass knew that it had been something she and her mother wanted under the roof of the Senor Dios. She had been eager to bring him to the Hacienda with drawn curtains and locked doors. Then she had grown terrified.

The first flush of passion had gone from Bass now, leaving him cold, empty and cheated. Lying there now, he remembered the words her mother had spoken, when she spoke of Will Crawford. '—Red-headed Will Crawford broke every promise he made to Captain Clay McCoy and to his bride— It was not in the nature of that wild Texan to be broken or fenced in—'

Now Bass knew what he should have known all along. He had voiced no kind of promise to this girl. He had not even asked her to marry him. Everything had happened too swiftly, and no promise of marriage was ever asked or given. Small wonder this girl doubted him. Bass had taken everything for granted. He had acted like some ignorant stupid fool.

'I love you, Kit,' he whispered, dry-throated. 'With all that a man has in him that is honorable and decent. I have never told that to any woman. I swear to God and all that I hold in the way of honor, that I will love and cherish you always, as long as I have life on earth. It was in my heart there in the mission. I should have spoken then, so that your mother could hear and understand.'

Tears dimmed Kit's eyes when he had finished. Her hands reached out and took his face, and she kissed him gently. Then she moved away from him and off the divan.

Bass lay there, her tears on his face, as he stared, unseeing into the darkness, recalling the promises he had just made this girl, and wondering if he would ever be able to keep them, remembering with an empty coldness inside him that he was an outlaw, a renegade, and that marriage ties of any kind were impossible. A few years at the most, and Bass Slocum would be dead, 'dobe-walled, or inside a Texas prison, waiting to be hanged for killing a Texas Ranger. Realization of what he had done, the enormity of his spoken promises that he could never keep, came to him now. His fists clenched, then he was on his feet, shaking his head as if to clear his brain.

Bass was too filled with contempt and hatred for himself to speak. He moved toward the door, to find Kit standing there, her arms reaching out for him.

'No.' His voice was harsh, ugly in the dark. 'I lied, Kit. This is not for us. I'm an outlaw, a renegade. Your mother will understand what I'm trying to tell you. It's no good, Kit.'

'Mama and I talked it over,' Kit said. 'She knows we are here alone together. She understands, and I understand. You didn't lie, Bass.' It was the girl who now pleaded as she clung to him, her weight dragging him away from the door.

Bass was holding her, fighting back all that was inside him. His words were barely audible. 'Our love will have to wait, Kit.' His face was in her hair. 'For a long time, perhaps forever. I am going back to Texas to face the man who gave me his name and raised me. I'm giving myself up to Captain Clay McCoy of the Texas Rangers, to stand trial for the murder of the man I shot and killed. I've got to clean my slate, regardless of whether I hang or go to the pen. That's my job, and the sooner I tackle it, the qiucker it'll be over and done with, one way or the other. If and when I'm a free man, I'll keep every promise I made you. I hope you can understand, Kit.'

Her lips met his in answer. 'I do, and I can wait, Bass. Now hold me for a while, until it is time for both of us to go. You and your Texans to round up the cattle, while I go with my mother and the Mexican families. This is our one night together, perhaps the only night we will ever know. We've given each other something to cherish and hold in our hearts. Hold me closer, Bass. I need your strength.'

As his arms closed her in, Bass tortured himself with the exquisite pain of her nearness, thinking this girl belonged to him and to him alone, letting the spent emotions ebb slowly back as his hands caressed her. It seemed like some dream to be remembered.

Bass was only half-aware of the blurred confusion of sounds outside as the Mexican families prepared for the evacuation of the only home they had ever had. To the younger generation, it was an exciting adventure. There was a feverish gaiety in the sounds of the younger voices. The giggling of a group of girls passing, snatches of little ranchero songs, the voices of lovers who paused in the deep shadows for hasty embrace.

There were the distant sounds of men's voices as they packed the wagons and carretas with their worldly goods. The cry of a baby being hushed at its mother's breast, the sobbing of the women who were leaving their homes behind them. Now and then the voice of Yaqui, harsh-sounding, as he barked some order to his men.

A group of Texans rode past, a little drunk, hoorawing one another with rough joshing, cussing their lack of women.

Through the blurred confusion came the voice of Dona Catalina, as she consoled the older women in their sorrow, or hushed the frightened whimpering of some child. Hearing her quiet voice, Bass had a sense of guilt as he held Kit in his arms.

There was a faint noise outside the barred window that was heavily draped. Kit's arms were around Bass' neck as he held her tensely, listening. The slim length of her body, warm and vibrant, moved against him, her quick, hot breath in his face, her amber eyes glazed with desire.

'Hola!' Yaqui's voice rasped outside. 'Vamos, hombre!'

There were the blurred sounds of a scuffle, the spatting of a hard slap.

'Yaqui, cabron!' That was Pablo talking. 'Be gone yourself, you nameless Yaqui cabron. I have business here. Give me back my gun.'

'Outside the Senorita's window.' Yagui's voice was dangerous, heavy with mockery. 'What kind of business that calls for a gun?'

'The gun was for the gringo Tejano cabron. He's inside the house, in the room with the Senorita.'

The sharp, spatting slap came again, and Pablo's tipsy voice, thick with anger said, 'Lay your filthy hand on me once more, you damn Yaqui and I'll kill you!'

Bass moved to the window, his gun in his hand. He pulled the heavy drapes aside. Tense with anger inside, he needed no man to take up his quarrel, but Yaqui and the jealous, drunken Pablo were already moving away.

'The Dona Catalina is concerned about you, Pablo,' Yaqui was saying as he prodded Pablo in the back with Pablo's own gun. 'She is there beside the campfire. Take your gun and give her an account of your actions, and be thankful you still have your life in you, hombre.'

Bass watched Pablo join the vaqueros who had come back with him, but Yaqui was no longer in sight. Bass turned slowly to find Kit standing a few feet behind him. The picture she made in the pale shaft of moonlight, her red hair tumbled down below her waist, her eyes shining, her red lips parted, was a vision that Bass would carry with him always, forever, wherever his dangerous trail might lead, to conjure up at night or in the dying embers of some campfire, perhaps even into death.

Bass let the heavy drapes drop back into place, leaving the room in darkness once more. 'It is time for me to get going,' Bass said abruptly, breaking the spell. 'It'll be daylight in half an hour.'

The tightness was back inside his belly, his nerves again keyed for danger. He was thinking he would have to kill Pablo, and he had a dread for the job. He wanted to kill no man, nor to have his own blood stain this early dawn. It was time he pulled out with his Texans, before something happened here.

'God protect you and bring you back to me,' Kit whispered.

They moved quickly to the front door. Kit put the key in the lock and let Bass out, closing the door quietly behind him.

Bass stumbled across the worn tiles of the patio. He was near the heavy, closed gates when a ruckus just outside pulled him up short. He opened the gates cautiously, just far enough to slide through. Half a dozen saddled horses stood back in the shadows, bridle reins dropped, ground tied.

Bass' Texans surrounded the giant Yaqui, who stood head and shoulders above the tallest of them. Yaqui's big hands were lifted to the level of his rawboned shoulders. His hat lay in the dust, and his thick black hair was sweat-matted. His eyes looked cold and hard. When he saw Bass standing in the narrow opening of the gates, his teeth bared. It could have been a grin or a snarl.

'We found this jasper alongside the gate, layin' for you, Bass,' said one of the Texans. He held the Luger in his hand.

'Turn him loose.' Bass took the Luger and put it in Yaqui's hand. Yaqui shoved the pistol into its scabbard. 'Yaqui will do to take along,' Bass told his men.

Yaqui's faded cotton shirt had come open. Bass could see the bone-white scar of the Big C that Pablo's father had branded there, on the dark-skinned, hairless chest. His opaque black eyes looked into the puckered gray eyes of Bass, and Bass thought he read something in the way of understanding there.

'Is there anything wrong here, Bass?' Dona Catalina asked, as she came out of the shadows.

'My men made a mistake,' Bass said. 'They figured Yaqui was aimin' to bushwhack me. I set 'em right.'

Bass cut a look at the giant who had picked his sombrero off the ground. It was back on his head now, the wide brim shadowing his black eyes and the wooden expression of his lean, dark face.

Dona Catalina spoke to Yaqui in his own language, and he gave her a brief reply in the same tongue.

'Yaqui was guarding the gate until you came out, Bass,' she explained. 'Your remuda and pack outfit are ready. Your pack mules are loaded with everything you'll need—grub, bedrolls, a keg of tequila. You know the trail to the upper valley claimed by the Alemanes, where the cattle are being held?'

Bass nodded, and asked, 'How long will it take you to move these families across the Rio Grande into Texas?'

'It's a fifty-mile trail from here, Bass. We'll only stop long enough to change teams and shift the packs to fresh mules. We should average five miles an hour. Add two or three hours for time out to change horses. We should be across the river before sunrise tomorrow morning at the very latest, providing we fight our way through any rebels on the prowl. Yaqui will have a hundred armed men along to fight them off.'

'When do you figure on starting?' Bass asked.

'About an hour from now,' came the quick

reply. 'About sunrise.'

'In broad daylight?' Bass spoke harshly. 'An outfit like this is the kind of pickin's Lobo Jones and his curly wolves are waitin' for. Guzman has half a dozen raidin' parties out. Once they sight this slow-movin' wagon train, they'll gang up. You'll have to fight every mile of it.

'Lay over here till dark,' Bass advised. 'Then pull out, an' keep movin' as fast as your outfit can travel. Me and my Texans will head Lobo Jones and his wolf pack to hell and gone, along with any Aleman raiders. When word gets to Lobo Jones and General Guzman that Bass Slocum an' his border jumpers are comin' after the cattle he's holdin' in the upper valley, Guzman will have every man he's got there to see that his big herd don't get stolen. I'll gamble all I got to lose that it works.

'You pull out with your wagon train tonight after dark, Kate,' Bass urged. 'You'll be across the Rio Grande some time tomorrow morning. I'll give you plenty of time to get across with your outfit before we let up pesterin' Lobo Jones' wolves and Guzman's Alemanes like a swarm of yellowjacket hornets.' Bass spilled tobacco into a brown wheatstraw paper and rolled and lit a cigarette.

'I understand,' Yaqui spoke up. 'Good. 'Sta Bueno, Bass Tejano. Like a Yaqui trick.'

'It will work all right, Bass, for me,' Dona Catalina said. 'But you'll be shot down, you and your men, while we'll be safe across the Rio Grande on Texas soil. I won't let you take that gamble at odds a hundred-to-one. I won't have your blood on my hands. I won't do it, Bass.'

'We've been up against the same odds for a year, Kate. You don't want these Mexican families slaughtered by El Lobo or Guzman's Alemanes. It's the only way to get you and Kit safe into Texas,' Bass said as he mounted a big palomino horse with the big C brand on his left shoulder. He spoke to Yaqui. 'You see to it, Yaqui, that this outfit stays here till after dark tonight.'

Yaqui's eyes glittered as he nodded.

One of his men came up. 'Pablo is gone,' he said to Dona Catalina, 'He took six men with him. He said to tell you he's joining El Lobo when the Texans come to get the cattle in the upper valley. He said that you had discharged him as Major Domo, and that Yaqui had given the Tejano Bass his string of palominos. That the Senorita had refused to marry him, and that the Tejano had spent the night with the Senorita. He said that—'

Yaqui lifted the Mexican off his feet, his big hands around the luckless man's throat.

'Set him down, Yaqui. The man is but the mouthpiece for Pablo,' Dona Catalina said quietly.

Dona Catalina looked up at Bass in the saddle and read embarrassment in his face.

Her hand reached up to cover Bass' hand where it lay on the saddle horn. 'God willing, I will see Captain Clay McCoy.' She spoke in a low tone. 'I have much to tell him, Bass.'

Bass had leaned a little forward to catch her words. The woman took his face in her hands and kissed him. It was a hard kiss that bruised her lips. Her eyes were tear-dimmed.

Bass straightened in his saddle. He looked at Yaqui and into his black eyes and found what he wanted there.

'With Pablo carryin' the mail,' Bass told his Texans, 'we're all set and ready to go. Let's get movin'.' He buckled on his old bullhide chaps that lay across the saddle, and lifted his hat in a farewell gesture.

'Vaya con Dios! Adios!' Dona Catalina called after them as they left. 'Muy hombre! Bass Tejano!' said Yaqui, his teeth bared.

'There's nothin',' said one of the Texans as they fell in behind the remuda and pack mules, 'like bitin' off a hell of a big chunk of raw meat. I shore take pity on them nibblers, like they had no appetite whatever.'

'Whoever said that a sorry, lovesick feller lost his appetite, never met Bass Slocum. The locoed Texican son-of-a-bitch has a dozen two-bit bastards like himself, and he's matched us agin' the damned Aleman army,' voiced another.

'Yeah,' spoke another. 'Shore prideful thataway. He takes on the whole damn

Aleman army before breakfast, gets the wrinkles outa his belly, takes five for a siesta, and cuts down the Federalists before bedtime. Don Bassito is muy hombre.'

'Big-hearted to boot,' said another man. 'Givin' away guns like he was passin' around stick candy to kids. Same way with wet cattle. Trouble is the bossman's still a kid. Some fellers is shaped like that. They never grow up. Like to play gun-tag with one and all.'

It was rough joshing, their cowpuncher way of hoorawing a man, and Bass knew better than to resent any of it. After a time they would tire of the game and drop it.

Actually, Bass was not paying too much attention to the banter that passed along with the tequila. When the bottle came into his hand, he took a stiff drink and passed it on to the next man. This was their way of letting Bass know that they were behind him, backing his play, and it pleased their Texan pride to go up against odds that no breed of men other than cowhands and Texans would think of tackling. They had confidence in themselves and in their leader, and the danger of the heavy odds added zest to the hazardous game.

Bass was not lacking in self-confidence, but he knew better than to discount odds. The undertaking at hand amounted to far more than helping Dona Catalina get her Santa Catalina Mexicans across the border, or getting Kit out of a dangerous country, or getting the wet cattle across the river. Bass was trying to remember, to recollect in detail, all that he had heard about General Kurt Guzman, self-pronounced Jefe of the State in Mexico which he was claiming for his Alemanes, and the secret Aleman Plan to capture Texas and then the entire United States.

Bass was trying to remember what Captain Clay McCoy had told him about the Aleman Germans on both sides of the Rio Grande, and about a lot of smart Japanese among them at the colony in Mexico.

The big plan was to take all the country between the Rio Grande and the Nueces River in Texas. It was a lot of country, enough to give the Alemanes a toehold in Texas. The Ranger Captain had said there was plenty of money behind the plan, and it was being used where it did the most good. Any politicos the money could not buy, were 'dobe-walled or disappeared overnight. Most of the Alemanes were married or living with Mexican women, and the women talked about the plan to every Mexican with whom they came in contact.

Those who were simpatica to the plan got a hundred pesos when they took the Aleman oath of allegiance. It was said that every Aleman had the Iron Cross brand tattooed on him. Lobo Jones and his curly wolves were wearing the brand, and Guzman had a list of names a mile long in his files of Mexicans who were wearing it. They were by no means all the peon class either. Money talked in any man's language, whether in dollars or pesos.

Captain Clay McCoy had told Bass it was a big plan, big and dangerous as hell. Good people, as well as the mercenary type, had been fooled into supporting it and had gone hog wild over it. They were taking advantage of, and following in the wake of Pancho Villa's revolt.

'What's worrying you, Bass?' asked a rangy Texan called Studs, as he shoved the bottle at him.

'I was born and raised in Texas, the same as the rest of you fellows,' Bass said quietly. 'I got into a little trouble there and crossed the river into Mexico, but crossin' the river didn't change the color of my hide, or what I got under it. I'm still a Texan, an' I'll fight for Texas till they cut me down. I'm declarin' a one-man war against Guzman's Alemanes. You boys don't need to go along. I can't promise you anything but a hell of a lot of grief. We can't look for help from north of the border. As Texans we haven't got a foot to stand on below the line. It amounts to a hell of a lot more than shovin' a drive of wet dogies across the river to oblige a lady.

'We're outnumbered,' Bass went on. 'Sooner or later we'll get cut down, and I won't ask any man to 'dobe-wall himself.' Bass reined up. 'You boys can turn back from here, and no hard feelin's.'

'You talk,' said Studs, 'like you were the only Texan in the outfit. Let's hear no more of that damn nonsense. Drink up and pass the bottle, Bass!'

CHAPTER FOUR

The Texans were out of the valley by sunrise and into the broken hills. They followed no trail, but kept to the same northwesterly direction. The Big Bend in the Rio Grande lay that way, and the upper valley claimed by the Alemanes, was this side of the river. They were headed straight for the stronghold of the enemy, traveling in the open, for the most part, without effort of concealment. Bass and his Texans were the decoys for the refugees from the Santa Catalina Grant.

They sighted small groups of horsebackers on the skyline, flanking them as they traveled. Bunches of four, or six or ten riders, always too far distant for their identity to be determined.

Bass left half a dozen men to handle the remuda and pack outfit. He took the other six and rode ahead. They rode in pairs, fanned out a hundred yards apart.

Bass had a grizzled Texan who went by the name of Pecos with him, and they were half a mile in the lead of the others when they rode up on an adobe hut. Heavy brush all but hid the jacal. No trail led to it, and it was partly luck and partly because they were on the lookout for bushwhackers, that they discovered it. The brush was so dense for a hundred yards around the hut that it was impossible to ride a horse through. Bass and Pecos swung from their saddles, their carbines in their hands, and leaving their horses in the brush, made their way through the thorny catclaw and mesquite thicket, moving with the caution of big-game hunters. They were still quite a distance from the jacal, deep in the brush thicket, when Bass gripped his partner's arm. They froze in their tracks, ears strained to pick up the slightest sound.

It came to them now, clear-toned in its metallic sharpness, the clicking of a telegraph key. Out here, fifty-odd miles from nowhere below the border on the Santa Catalina Grant, was a telegraph key, clicking out some message, with no visible telegraph wires to carry the words.

The eyes of the two men met in puzzlement. Then Bass whispered, 'Morse code. We'd better split up, Pecos. Like as not there'll be a pair of 'em. We'll try to take at least one alive, so he can fetch us country boys up to date. Shoot to cripple your man.'

Bass was on his hands and knees, crawling through the underbrush, following the tunnel used by small animals. Fifty yards of crawling on his belly, with Pecos coming in from another angle, brought the small adobe jacal abruptly into Bass' vision. It was in the middle of a fifty-foot clearing. A thin wire was stretched between a pair of long split-bamboo poles with metal fittings at the joints, and the unpolished steel covered over with black paint to dull the telltale reflection of the sun. The twin poles reached to a height of fifty feet, and the almost invisible wire was stretched between them.

The mud jacal had no windows, but Bass could see the gunports in the twelve-inch adobe walls. The door was open, and a machine gun sat on a tripod in the doorway. A man squatted on the dirt floor of the hut, his back to the doorway and the machine gun. A polished mahogany box, with metal knobs and dials, rested on a rawhide-covered kyack box. The man who squatted, tailor-fashion, on the floor wore a set of earphones. He was sending a message from an open notebook on the floor alongside him, over a telegraph key.

Even as Bass watched, the man slipped off the earphones and got to his feet with the single unbroken movement of an acrobat. He flexed his legs a couple of times to get the kinks out, then twisted the two metal knobs on the wireless set, as he turned around to face the open doorway.

The man was Japanese. Short, stocky, with

black hair. He wore a loose-fitting cotton shirt, and the shirt tail hung out to cover the waistband of his wrinkled but clean khaki pants. He carried a Mauser automatic in a shoulder holster, with the gun under his left armpit. He was bare-footed, his heavy army shoes placed neatly alongside the kyack box.

The stocky Japanese stepped outside, lifting the loose shirt to scratch his belly while he looked around. He had stepped outside to look around cocking his head sideways as the earphones on the headset commenced to stutter out some message.

'Hands up!' Bass called out sharply. 'Or I'll gut-shoot you!'

The man's right hand, that he had been using to scratch his belly, snaked toward the Mauser. His eyes glittered as he looked toward the brush that hid Bass.

Bass thumbed back the hammer of his single-action Colt .45 and squeezed the trigger. The heavy slug tore through his victim's right shoulder, the force of it spinning him around. As the wounded man ran for the doorway, Bass shot him in one leg. The man staggered and fell, rolling over quickly toward the doorway and the safety of the cabin.

From inside the small jacal, another man appeared. He was crouched behind the machine gun, swinging it around on its tripod. He was a heavyset, red-faced man with roached blond hair. Bass flattened himself against the ground as the machine gun rattled, the burst of gunfire sending a spray of bullets above him into the dense brush thicket.

The sharp crack of a 30-30 carbine sounded from the brush, off to Bass' left. The machine gun stopped, the heavy barrel tilted upward at the sky. The big blond man lay sprawled on his face, his heavy body blocking the doorway, his roached hair sodden with blood from the bullet that had shattered his skull.

The wounded telegrapher was crawling crab-wise toward the cabin now. Bass lurched to his feet, his six-shooter in his hand. The telegrapher had a hand grenade in his left hand and was pulling the pin with his teeth, when Bass' gun barrel chopped down across his skull. Bass jerked the hand grenade from the victim's hand and flung it as far as he could, ducking the explosion. Through its echoes and falling debris, Pecos charged out of the brush and into the cabin.

When Bass came into the cabin, Pecos had the notebook in his hands, cursing tonelessly. 'Most of it's in German and Japanese hen-scratchin', Bass,' Pecos said. 'I hope you left enough life in that critter for a man to work on. I had to kill the Aleman machine gunner. We'd better look the varmint over for pineapples. That crazy bastard will blow us up and himself to boot.'

Bass found two more hand grenades in the telegrapher's belt, under his shirt tails. He carried the deadly little Mauser and the hand grenades inside and laid them on the kyack box.

Pecos found a quart bottle with a Japanese label on it. He pulled the cork and sniffed the contents. 'It's a booze called Saki,' Pecos said. 'Those guys use it for a brave-maker.'

Pecos grabbed the telegrapher by his hair and shoved the neck of the bottle between the man's teeth. 'Drink hearty, you son-of-a-bitch, or I'll shove the bottle neck down your throat and bust it off.'

The man's frightened eyes looked from a wooden mask as he swilled the potent rice liquor until the bottle was pulled away.

'Tell us what that wireless outfit's sayin', before I commence lookin' for head lice with this.' Pecos lit a match and singed the man's hair. If he felt pain, the man gave no outward sign. The Texan cursed him.

Bass was exploring the jacal. He found the bedroll where the Aleman had been sleeping, the telegrapher's blanket rolled in another corner, and enough grub to last two men for a month in kyack boxes. Another kyack held about a dozen bottles of Saki and the colorless, potent kummel, with a German label. There were spare parts for the machine gun, half a dozen Mauser rifles, and enough ammunition for all the guns to supply a small army.

It was not until Bass' bootheel accidentally caught in an iron ring about the size of a cinch ring, buried in the hard-packed dirt floor, that he found anything important. The ring was fastened to a trap door, about three feet square.

'Could be I've struck paydirt,' Bass called to Pecos as he opened the trap door.

The wireless had quit sputtering. Bass had found a flashlight and shot its yellow light into the ten-foot square cellar; a four-runged ladder led down into it. He could see boxes of ammunition piled high and stacks of guns in packing boxes. He also saw a little hill of paper-backed pamphlets, neatly piled and three wireless sets in crates, complete with the jointed bamboo poles and coiled wire.

'I'm going down to look it over,' Bass said. 'You stand guard up here, Pecos. Some of the boys will show up directly. That hand grenade was loud enough to fetch them on the run. This little jacal was headquarters for something.'

Bass skimmed through the pamphlets, printed in Spanish. They gave the outline of the Aleman Plan, setting forth the advantages of the plot to take Texas and use it for an opening wedge to take the whole United States, parceling it out to the Mexicans and the Japanese who were proved loyal to the plan. The reward for that loyalty was astounding. It would make every one involved in it a rich man. Bass shoved some of the pamphlets into his pockets and searched further.

He found some code books, compact and in detail. The German words were translated into Japanese, Spanish and English for the benefit of gringo traitors to the United States, fugitives below the border who had joined the Alemanes. A second book listed all enemies to be killed. Bass found his name in the latter book, together with the names of his Texans.

Bass put both books in his pocket. He found a pair of saddlebags and filled them with what he wanted in the way of information and proof against the Aleman Plan. Then he climbed the ladder.

Pecos had broken the seal on a bottle of kummel and was sampling the stuff that had the taste of caraway seed. He motioned with the bottle, through the open doorway, where his Japanese captive lay in a doubled-up position against the door. His head was lobbed forward and his hands held against his belly. The ivory hilt of the long knife embedded in his belly, just below the brisket, was held in a death grip by the brown hands that were staining crimson.

'Hari-kari,' Pecos said. 'He was looking into my eyes when he slid that toad stabber plumb into his guts, gizzard, lights and heart. He never batted an eye till his head drooped over. Shows what that Saki can do.'

Pecos held out the bottle to Bass. 'Try a horn of this Aleman juice. It'll put kinks in that hair you're wearin'.'

Bass' Texans were breaking trail through the brush. Bass and Pecos stepped outside to meet them.

'It'd be too much to expect,' Bass said, as the men drew up before him, 'that there's a man among you that savvies a wireless outfit.'

'I took a course in telegraphy at night school,' spoke a young Texan called Beans, because he was forever asking when it was time to eat. 'It's been a long time—'

He swung from his saddle as the telegraph key started its stuttering. Squatting on his bootheels, the headset on, he jotted down the message as it came through. When the wireless went silent, he scowled at what he had written down, his eyes puzzled.

'Must be some foreign lingo,' Beans told Bass. 'We'll have to capture us a live Aleman to interpret it, but it was in Morse Code, for sure.'

'We got somethin' big here, boys,' Bass said. 'But we don't know what to do with it and we can't hang around long enough to get the swing of it.'

Beans cocked his head sideways, listening. He slipped on the headset. 'It's a code station,' he said. 'Number One.'

Bass thumbed through one of the code books he had found. 'Number One is Alemanda,' he said. 'It's a town in the upper valley, down the river from Hidalgo, Guzman's headquarters.' Bass' grin left his eyes hard and cold as old ice.

'Want to send a message to Butcher Guzman or Lobo Jones, while the line's open?' Beans asked.

'Hell yes,' Bass said. 'Tell the sonsabitches that Bass Slocum and his Texans have taken over this jacal. We found what was down the cellar, an' we're using everything there to our advantage. Tell 'em that we're gatherin' the Santa Catalina cattle Lobo Jones is holding, an' we're shovin' the big herd across the Rio Grande into Texas.'

Bass paused while the sandy-haired Beans tapped out the message and nodded for Bass to continue.

'Tell Guzman,' Bass said, 'and Lobo Jones that Bass Slocum an' his Texans have declared open season on any man wearin' the Aleman Iron Cross. We'll shoot 'em down where we find 'em, an' all hell can't stop us.' Bass thumbed back his hat while Beans clicked out the message.

Beans grinned widely and said, 'I signed it "Bass Slocum McCoy and all Texans in Mexico."'

Beans removed the headset to keep the deafening static that started coming in, from his ears. It sounded like a bunch of firecrackers exploding.

'Sounds like the damn outfit's about to blow up,' said Bass.

'That's some powerful wireless station

cuttin' in,' said Beans.

The static broke off abruptly. Beans adjusted the headset with one hand and grabbed up his pencil to catch the message that was coming in on the telegraph key.

Bass leaned over to read the message Beans was scribbling down. '"Good hunting, Bass,"' he read aloud. '"You won't be short-handed when you wet your Santa Catalina cattle in the Rio Grande. The eyes of Texas are upon you, and may God ride with you Texans. This is the Ranger Station at Palofox. Captain Clay McCoy sent this message. Palofox signing off."'

Beans slid the headset from his sweat-damp, sandy hair. 'That was your old man, Bass,' he said in an awed tone.

Bass nodded. A lump had come up into his throat, and he dared not trust his voice. It felt like the hard lump he had carried inside him all these long, bitter months had burst and spilled its warmth inside him.

'Captain Clay McCoy?' The grizzled Pecos lifted the bottle of kummel in his hand. 'By God, there's a man you kin tie to!' He took a big swallow and handed it to the sunburnt Beans. It was a prayer, rather than profanity, in his voice.

The bottle made its rounds. There were three fingers left in it when Pecos handed it to Bass. Bass drained what was left.

Bass had found a pair of German-made

binoculars in a leather case. He focused them now on a brush-covered ridge and swept its length. A group of riders came into view, and he studied them for a few minutes before he lowered the glasses.

'There's about fifty horsebackers, he called out to his men. 'They're headin' this way. If I had one guess, I'd say it was Aleman cavalry on the prowl. They're flyin' some kind of a flag. They're about a mile away.'

'Mebbyso,' Pecos said as he stepped out of the hut. 'It's one of these. I took it off the dead critter here,' he said, indicating the telegrapher. Pecos held up a silk flag, about two feet square. The background was a vivid yellow. In the center was a circle of solid red, with a black Iron Cross marked in the red circle. It bore the label, 'Made in Japan.'

No man there had ever seen such a flag. It was Bass who gave his own interpretation of its meaning. Red and yellow were the rebel colors of Pancho Villa. The Villistas had a plain red and yellow pennant under which they fought.

The red sun of Japan was on the Villista yellow. The Aleman Iron Cross was on the Jap red-sun emblem.

'Do we carry the fight to 'em? Or make our stand here?' Pecos asked.

'I got what I want in these saddlebags,' Bass said. 'You fellows help yourselves to what you feel like takin' along, because we're movin' pronto to set a bushwhacker trap for the

Alemanes.'

Bass went back inside the cabin and down into the cellar with his flashlight. 'Them as is squeamish,' he called up, 'had better start workin' on that Saki firewater. This ain't goin' to be a purty sight. Lend a hand with this box of dynamite.'

Bass handed up a case of dynamite and a box of caps, then a detonator, fashioned like a tire pump, and a coil of insulated copper wire.

'Get that Station One, Beans,' Bass said as he climbed up the ladder. 'Tell 'em that we're about to blow a hundred head of Alemanes into hell. After you send the message, smash the wireless outfit.'

'I'd shore like to take this wireless set along, Bass,' Beans said. 'This is about the finest set made, and these rawhide kyacks are special made to pack it on a mule. It could come in handy. What do you say I take it, Bass?'

'There's one of 'em already packed and ready to load, complete with the wire and fish poles, down in the cellar. A couple of you fellers fetch it up and load it on a mule, while the hungry Beans gets a rise outa this wireless outfit.'

Beans nodded and grinned as he fingered the telegraph key, speaking the message aloud as he tapped it out.

'"Aviso! Take warning! Bass Slocum McCoy and his Texans are setting a dynamite trap for an Aleman patrol coming down the ridge. Half an hour from now their carcasses will be in small chunks, to make easy pickings for the buzzards. Here's hoping that Guzman and the mangy lobo wolf are getting this message direct. You have five minutes to put in your answer before we blow this place to hell along with the Aleman patrol."'

In less than a minute the answer came back. Bass leaned over to read it as Beans wrote it out. '"Aviso! Take warning Bass Slocum. Before you carry out your gringo Tejano threat to destroy Aleman property and kill that patrol, be advised and warned of this: That the Dona Catalina and her young and beautiful daughter are still in Mexico and are at the mercy of General Kurt Guzman, Jefe and Dictator of Alemanda."'

Beans jerked the headset from his sweat-matted, sand-colored head. 'The slimy sonofabitch runs one hell of a big bluff, Bass.'

'It's Bass Slocum who's runnin' the bluff, feller,' Bass said grimly. 'With a little old stack of dirty white chips and drawin' cards to fill an inside flush.' He hitched up the cartridge belt that sagged across his lean flanks. 'I could use a good powder man,' Bass said as he picked up the coil of insulated wire.

'I'm your huckleberry.' Pecos had the detonator in his hand. 'Where do you want the powder? You got enough dynamite sticks in that box to blow up half of Mexico.'

'We'll bunch 'em around the jacal.' Bass'

eyes were slivers of steel. 'Corral 'em in with powder.'

Bass told the rest of his men to ride out a ways and bush up, while he and Pecos attended to the dynamite. 'You ride herd on your wireless set, Beans,' Bass said. 'Have it tuned to sing a death chant. Git goin'.'

CHAPTER FIVE

There was something pitifully ludicrous about the Aleman rebel cavalry as it came into sight along the narrow trail that twisted through the brush thicket. They were a bunch of run-of-the-mill rag-tag rebel soldiers, outfitted in obsolete uniforms, purchased in wholesale lot from Bannerman's. Their second-hand, dirty, gray-wool uniforms, with red facings on the blouse and broad red stripes down the pants, were war surplus from some past European war. The dingy red caps had a black replica of the Iron Cross stitched above the cracked patent leather peaks, and the outmoded knapsacks on their backs dated the uniforms that fit like gray sacking on these under-sized, half-starved men.

None of the men wore shoes. Only crude-thonged cowhide sandals were strapped on dirty feet. The second-hand, regulation U.S. Cavalry McClellan saddles, fitted with empty carbine boots, were cinched around the bellies of skinny cayuses and old mules. These raw recruits carried no firearms. The heavy-bladed peon machetes, used in the fields, were shoved, naked-bladed, into the black belts that came with the uniforms. These were the typical 'dobe soldiers of Mexico, blood-brothers to the Federalistas under the command of the late El Capitan Vidal.

There were a dozen Aleman soldiers, with the corporal and sergeant stripes of non-commissioned officers on the sleeves of their dingy gray blouses. These noncoms were heavily armed with carbines and Mauser pistols, cross belts, bristling with brass cartridges, across their breasts. These men were of larger stature, who fit their blouses till the seams were stretched to the breaking point, and the buttons threatened to pop. Blond, red-faced and sweating, brutality stamped on their faces, these men were foot soldiers who sat awkwardly in their saddles, shifting uneasily to ease the bothersome pain of saddle boils.

At the head of this nondescript cavalcade rode a heavy-built man in a tailored gray uniform and thick, black boots that came to his knee joints. His square, brutish face was an oily, yellowish, muddy color, almost the same color of his cropped hair and the thin line of mustache on his short upper lip. Even his bloodshot eyes had taken on the same muddy tone, to blend cameo-like with the rest of his coloring. There were four gun-metal pips on his shoulder strap, to give him the rank of Colonel. His red cap with the black Iron Cross insignia, sat at a rakish angle, so that the patent leather peak slanted across one eye. Arrogance and a ruthless brutality were there, in every gesture.

Behind this Aleman Colonel, rode Pablo, late Major Domo of the Santa Catalina Grant. Pablo was the only horseman of the lot, and he sat his silver-crusted Mexican saddle with a certain swagger, a sullen look in his eyes as he spurred his horse up alongside the colonel's mount.

Bass, after a start of surprise at thus seeing Pablo, dismissed him. Pablo's saddle gun scabbard was empty. The silver-handled six-shooter was no longer there in its carved scabbard. It looked as if Pablo was a prisoner.

'Gott in Himmel!' The colonel let out an explosive grunt.

Bass moved into the doorway, the cigarette still in the corner of his mouth. The six-shooter in his hand was pointed at the belly of the Aleman colonel.

'Take it easy, Aleman,' Bass called out. 'If this gun goes off, there'll be a hell of a hole in your guts.'

Bass spoke to Pablo. 'You might come in handy, Pablo, when we 'dobe-wall these Alemanes. You can pick out a dozen of the 'dobe recruits, an' I'll pass out the guns they were brought here to get. It don't make much difference about their bein' crack shots. There's plenty of ammunition here. You're just the hombre we need to boss the firin' squad.'

Bass motioned with his six-shooter to the colonel. 'Step down, Buster!'

The colonel's face was a sweat-slicked, jaundiced yellow. He kept wetting his lips as he sat stolidly in his saddle.

Bass' gun spit a jet of flame. The heavy .45 slug tore the red cap from the colonel's head. 'I told you to step down,' Bass said. 'The next bullet will bust that axle-greased thick head you got on your neck!'

The colonel dismounted hastily. He had his hands raised to the level of his shoulders as he planted both feet on solid ground.

'He's Colonel Noel Guzman,' volunteered Pablo. 'Only son of General Kurt Guzman, Jefe of Alemanda.'

'The hell!' Bass grinned. 'Your old man's just been burnin' the wireless.'

The colonel looked at Bass with muddy, venomous eyes.

'Beans, get that wireless outfit warmed up,' Bass called out. 'Pecos, you and the boys take them tin soldiers off their played-out nags. Shoot 'em loose if they don't savvy.'

Bass' eyes flicked back to the colonel. 'Step inside, Buster, an' I hope you make a move for that Luger you got on your fat rump.'

Bass prodded the bulky colonel with his gun barrel. He made him step across the bodies of the dead Japanese and the Aleman machine gunner.

'Stand over in the corner, Buster,' Bass ordered. 'You can be thinkin' up a dying message for your old man while the wireless outfit is warmin' up.'

'I have nothing to say.' Colonel Noel Guzman stood stiffly, clicking his heels together to stand at attention. His bloodshot, muddy eyes were glazed with hate and the murderous humiliation of his capture. He was breathing heavily through hairy nostrils and a half-opened mouth. His dank, roached hair stood out like the bristles on a hog.

Bass eyed the man with contempt and suspicion as he saw his pudgy fingers fumble at his holster flap. When the colonel pulled the Luger out with a deliberate slowness, Bass thumbed back the hammer of his Colt .45. Guzman's thick lips thinned in a faint sneer as he took the Luger by the barrel and held it out, butt toward the Texan, in a formal gesture of military surrender. He clicked his bootheels and bowed stiffly.

'Colonel Noel Guzman,' he said in a guttural voice, 'surrenders. I demand the courtesy shown to a prisoner of war.'

Bass stared at the man, then at the gun in his hand. He shoved his six-shooter into the holster tied down on his thigh, and without warning, slapped the Luger out of the colonel's hand.

'Sit down, you slimy, stinkin' son-of-a-bitch.' Bass had all his weight behind the fist that he buried, wrist-deep, in the pit of Guzman's paunch. Guzman's muddy eyes rolled back to show the bloodshot whites as he doubled up and landed with a heavy thud on the hard-packed dirt floor. The far wall held him there in a slumped sitting posture.

Bass was breathing hard as he stood over the man who was gasping for breath. 'I never put the boots to a man yet,' Bass gritted. 'But I'm shore as hell tempted to kick your teeth down your throat, you goose-steppin' military bastard!'

'I got the Aleman station, Bass,' the lanky sunburnt Beans grinned.

Bass bared his teeth in a grin that left his eyes cold as ice, and said, 'Tell General Butcher Guzman that we got a tub of guts here who claims to be Colonel Noel Guzman. Tell the Butcher that I'm keepin' his slimy son on ice till I get word that Dona Catalina and her daughter are safe and unharmed on their Texas ranch.'

Bass rolled and lit a cigarette while he waited for Guzman's reply. It did not take long to come in.

'General Guzman wants proof of his son's identity, Bass,' Beans said, reading what he had written down.

'Ask him if he wants just the head,' Bass said flatly, 'or the whole carcass.' He struck a match on the colonel's boot and relit his cigarette. 'Tell the Aleman I got the deal, an' I'm playin' for keeps.'

Bass spat the half-smoked cigarette into the colonel's face. 'Prisoner of war!' He shoved his foot into the brass-buttoned paunch. 'Nuts!' The colonel quivered but said nothing.

Bass stepped into the doorway while Beans was sending the message. A train of pack mules was coming in now. Two Aleman sergeants were in command of a squad of 'dobe soldiers.

There were probably twenty women camp-followers with the pack train that the Texans were herding into the clearing. All of the women were very young, the average age no more than seventeen. Some were on foot, and some rode mules. They had the beaten, sullen look of prisoners. They were bareheaded, barefooted, their only garment a dirty, ragged cotton dress, a sleeveless sack that showed the bare legs of those on foot, the bare thigh of the more fortunate ones who rode bareback mules.

Bass' belly was still tied in a hard knot, his jaws clenched as he fought down the urge to kill Noel Guzman and then inform General Guzman of his son's death. His hatred and lust to kill came from a remark that Dona Catalina had made: 'Guzman wants to marry me, Bass, to get title to the Santa Catalina. He has a son who is a colonel and field officer in charge of his Aleman troops, and he is trying to force a marriage between his son and my daughter, who will own the Santa Catalina when I die. General Guzman and his son play all the angles, and Noel Guzman is even more rotten than his father.'

Bass had not revealed the source of the anger that had made him want to kill the Aleman colonel. He knew that the lanky Beans was wondering at his brutality to his prisoner.

The look of murder was in Bass' eyes now as he watched his Texans drag the two Aleman sergeants from their played-out horses. He heard Pecos telling the women camp-followers that they were free now, that there was a lot of canned goods in the cellar of the jacal, and that he would see to it that it was all fetched out before the hut was blown up.

'You gals just sit down and take it easy, till Bass Slocum gets his chores done,' Pecos said.

Bass saw one of the women slide off the back of a mule. She spoke to Pecos, who pointed to the jacal where Bass was standing, and she headed his way.

Bass watched her as she walked past the Aleman prisoners and the peons. There was something about this girl, the way she carried herself and her aloof contempt for the soldiers, that marked her. That barelegged girl in a rag of a dress was no pitiful peon girl. Bass saw her eye Pablo, who was squatted apart from the soldiers. He saw her toss her head, shaking back the long, black hair. He heard her low-toned voice as she spat the single word at him. 'Cabron!'

Bass watched the litheness of her movements as her bare feet stepped clear of the blood that puddled around the dead Japanese. She was standing almost within his reach now, a slender, long-legged girl, with olive-tinted skin and clear-cut, delicate features. She was looking at him with dark-brown eyes, her heavy black brows lifted, her lips twisted in a quizzical half-smile. There was something familiar about the girl. Bass was trying to place her when her lips peeled back from startlingly white teeth. Bass flinched inside at the brittle sound of her laugh. She broke it off abruptly.

'I'm not blaming you, Bassito.' She spoke with a slight accent in a throaty voice. 'I'd refuse to recognize Pepa.'

'Pepa!' Bass reached out for her, but she backed away quickly. 'Pepa,' he said. 'Pepita. Good God! What have they done to you, youngster?'

'God had nothing to do with what you see, Bassito. God sleeps at night at Alemanda. It is Don Diablo, the devil that comes to the cantina to listen to Pepa sing and dance for Don Diablo, who has taken the name and shape of Colonel Noel Guzman.'

Memory of this girl came back with sudden clarity. Her gay laughter, her little ranchero songs in the candlelight as she perched herself on his table in a far corner of the patio at the Cantina Laredo, laughter in her eyes, teasing him with the promise of her red lips.

She shook her head, backing away from Bass who had taken a step toward her. 'No, Bassito. Don't touch me. I'm as filthy inside as this dirty rag he threw at me to cover myself when I refused to dance the goose step for the drunken son of a dog and his Aleman soldiers last night.' Her brown eyes blazed now.

'When Pablo rode into camp, I thought he had come to take me away,' she said. 'That Major Domo was forever showing me his six-shooter with the silver handle, bragging how many enemies he had killed, swearing his love for me by the gun that had been handed down to him by his father and his father's father. For a brave and fearless caballero, he gave up the beautiful gun that he had cut his baby teeth on far too quickly and easily. He gave away the most valued thing he owned, without argument. That Pablo cabron sat there and drank from any bottle passed to him, while he watched those little peon girls perform for the drunken borracho Aleman soldiers, who forced tequila down their throats.'

'It's all over now, Pepita,' Bass told the girl. 'The sooner you forget what happened, the better off you'll be.' He forced a mirthless grin. 'I know that sounds silly as hell.'

'I don't want to forget any part of it, Bassito. They were bringing these recruits here to give them guns and ammunition. They were going to tattoo the Aleman Iron Cross on their chests. The Aleman son of a dog told me what he was going to have the artist put on my body.'

'Listen, Pepita, it's over. What you need is a hot bath and warm grub and clothes. Then we'll see about getting you and these girls across the border,' Bass told her quietly. When he reached out and took the girl's hand, she made no effort to pull away.

'What are you going to do with Noel Guzman and his men?' she asked, her dark eyes narrowing.

'I'm keeping the colonel alive for a while. I reckon we'll 'dobe-wall the gringo Alemanes and turn the peons loose.'

'Pablo?' she asked. 'What becomes of the brave Major Domo cabron?'

'Quien sabe? Hard to say,' Bass said grimly. 'I'll talk it over with him later. I'll use him to pick out some 'dobe soldiers for a firing squad to 'dobe-wall the Alemanes, to give the commands.'

The girl freed her hand. She stepped past him and picked up the Luger Bass had knocked from Guzman's hand, into the puddle of drying blood. Bass went a little sick inside when she cleaned the red muck from the gun on her rag of a dress. The look in her eyes made him shiver.

'How about Pepita giving the commands to the firing squad?' The toneless voice matched the look in her eyes. She balanced the Luger in her hand. 'I've got more right to the job than Pablo.' She looked through the doorway to where Noel Guzman sat on the floor with his back against the wall.

Bass took hold of the girl's hand that gripped the Luger, shoving the gun barrel down. 'I want him kept alive until I'm through dickering with General Kurt Guzman. When I'm done usin' the stinkin' tub of guts, I'll hand him over to you. That's a promise, Pepita.' His arm was across the girl's shoulders.

'I'll hold you to it, Bass McCoy.' She tried to shrug away from his arm. 'I'm filthy dirty,' she said in a gritty voice. 'Inside and outside.'

'Not to my notion, you're not,' Bass told her, a faint grin on his face. 'There's nothin' wrong with you that soap and hot water won't clean off.'

'It's on the inside, Bassito, where it won't scrub off,' Pepa said.

Beans was waving a message at Bass, a wide grin on his face. 'Aleman Jefe is guaranteeing the safety of Dona Catalina and her daughter across the Rio Grande. He's willin' to do anything in his power to get his son back, unharmed. He's still runnin' off at the head—

Cripes!' Beans jerked the headset off as the static cracked through the earphones.

The static cut off suddenly. The Ranger Station at Palofox was on the air now. 'Hang onto Colonel Noel Guzman till you hear from me. Ill let you know when the two ladies are safe. You got both Guzmans where you want them. Don't let go your handholt, Bass. Signed, Clay McCoy, Captain of the Texas Rangers.'

Beans read the message aloud, cutting covert glances at Pepa.

'I'll keep my promise to your old man,' Bass told the sweating colonel. 'But if the lady here empties that Luger into your tub of guts, it can't be helped, an' no Texan here is goin' to stop her if she takes the notion.'

The lanky Beans had taken off his headset and had gone down the ladder with a flashlight. He came up with a large bolt of yellow silk over his shoulder. He grinned as he handed it to Pepa. 'I remembered seein' it when I fetched up the wireless set. I reckon they aimed to make their flags out of it. It'll look better cut into a dress for you, ma'am.'

'Gracias, Tejano.' Pepa smiled faintly. 'If I wasn't so filthy dirty, I'd give you a hug and a kiss you'd remember.'

'You look all right to me, ma'am.'

'Her name,' grinned Bass, 'is Pepa. That's the only name she's got, so far as I know. Pepa. Pepita, if you get right chummy.' Bass motioned with his hand. 'This is Beans. Frijole Beans. Because he likes 'em, with or without trimmin's.'

'I could use a cake of soap and a towel, Beans,' Pepa told the sandy-haired Texan. 'After I've scrubbed up and dressed, I'll thank you more. I wonder if there's a needle and thread and scissors—'

Beans slid down the ladder. He came back up with a small box in his hand. 'Harness needles and thread aplenty.' He handed her the box, a grin spreading from ear to ear.

'Frijole Beanses,' Pepa said in her husky voice as she came close, a sparkle in her eyes that Bass had occasion to remember. 'That is a most beautiful name.'

She pulled Beans' head down to the level of hers and kissed him, stepping back before the lanky Texan recovered his balance. Her short laugh held a sob in it.

She whirled on her dancer's toes, the bolt of cloth, the square box, the Luger somehow in her arms, to stand in front of the Aleman colonel on the dirt floor. Lips pulled away from white teeth, she spat into his muddy eyes. 'Aleman gringo cabron!' she said, and slapped him, open-handed, back and forth, back and forth, till the print of her hand marked white against his mottled skin.

'Cabron, Aleman cabron, son of an Aleman dog!' Tears of anger filmed the hate in her dark eyes. Her voice choked in a sob as she shoved the barrel of the Luger into his slack-jawed mouth.

'Easy, Pepita!' Bass shoved his boot in the Colonel's sweat-slimed face, and the bullet head hit the wall. He took the gun from Pepa. 'Spit in his eyes, an' call it a day, kid. Next time you make up your mind to play for keeps, this is the safety.' He shoved her thumb against it.

Bass pushed the sobbing girl into Beans' awkward arms. 'Show her where the water hole is, Frijole Beanses,' he said. 'If she wants you to scrub her back, have at it. If you make time with Pepita, you'll be the first man—gringo, Aleman or Mex, who's ever made the grade. But if Pepita ever meets the hombre she wants, nothin' this side of hell will help him, and that lucky hombre will have hit the jackpot.'

'You say those things,' the girl's laughter hurdled a sob, 'to make Pepita feel happy once more. Look at me! Filthy pig of a javalina sow! You're making fun of Pepita!'

Bass grinned. That was more like the Pepita be remembered, the laughing, teasing, tormenting senorita, whose eyes and lips and songs promised everything this side of Paradise, and gave nothing when it came time to lay it on the line.

Bass shoved the girl and Beans out the door. He took the notebook from his pocket, and yanking the front of the colonel's blouse, he jerked the man up into a sitting position, and shoved the notebook into his hands. 'This is the last message your pardner there took down before he went to hell. Read it aloud.'

Noel Guzman stared down at the German words. He looked up at Bass, sullen-eyed, licking the blood from his bruised lips, and said harshly, 'The message is in code.'

Bass stepped to the door and beckoned Pecos. 'Buster has sulled,' Bass said. 'He claims the message was taken down in code.'

Pecos picked up a bottle of kummel and broke it on the adobe wall above the colonel's head. The shattered glass and the colorless liquor spilled down on the colonel's bare head, bits of glass sticking in the roached hair, while the liquor ran down across his face. Pecos held the jagged, broken bottle close to the man's face. 'How's this for a key to that code?' Pecos said flatly.

'Nein!' Guzman croaked, wiping his wet face with the palm of his hand. 'Gott in Himmel! Nein!' he screamed, covering his face and eyes with his hands.

Pecos tossed the broken bottle outside. 'Fetch in one of them Aleman bastards that was givin' up head,' he called to one of the Texans.

When a young towhead was shoved through the doorway, Bass saw the horror in his pale eyes as he looked at the colonel whose hands still covered his face. Bass picked up the notebook and handed it to the Aleman sergeant. 'Read it,' he said.

'"Colonel Noel Guzman,"' the sergeant began in a harsh whisper. '"Patrol Number One. Arm all recruits without delay. Proceed by forced march immediately to the Hacienda Santa Catalina. Wipe out resistance to the last man. Hold Dona Catalina and her daughter prisoners. Use your own methods to convince the girl. General Guzman will attend to her mother. Kill all men. Distribute the young women among the Alemanes. This is the beginning of our purge as planned.

'"The bandit, Bass Slocum and his men are in your vicinity. There's a big bounty on their carcasses. Collect it. Set up a wireless station at the Hacienda. Send me immediate information when you have carried out these orders to completion. Signed, General Kurt Guzman, Jefe of Alemanda"'

The blond sergeant, pale beneath his grimy face, avoided looking at the colonel as Bass took the notebook from his unsteady hands.

'Swinehund!' rasped Colonel Guzman. 'Pig of a dog!' His muddy eyes glared at the youthful sergeant.

Pecos grinned and shoved a bottle of kummel into the sergeant's hands, and pushed him out the door. The young man was sobbing and cursing as he stumbled away.

'That shore broke down the code, Buster,' Bass said. He turned to Pecos. 'Pass out guns and cartridges to the 'dobe peons. All the canned stuff and grub to the women. Hog-tie this tub of guts. I'm havin' a heart-to-heart talk with Pablo.'

Pecos pulled Pablo's silver-handled six-shooter from the waistband of his own levis and handed the gun, butt first, to Bass. 'I found it in the colonel's saddle pockets. It might come in handy, Bass.'

Bass had the fancy gun in his hand when he faced Pablo. Pablo had gotten to his feet and stood there, half-defiant.

'You still want to throw in with this Aleman outfit, Pablo?' Bass asked.

'Por Dios! No!' Pablo looked sick. 'It is as I tell these hombres. Those gringo Alemanes are dogs, dirty dogs!'

'Then go with these peons and the women,' Bass told him, speaking in a lowered tone. 'Dona Catalina leaves tonight, after dark. If you pull out now, you'll cut their trail some time tonight. Set all the women on the stoutest horses and mules. Let the men walk if their mounts play out.'

Bass handed Pablo his gun. 'Hang onto it, now you've got it back. Line up your men. You're in charge.'

The sun stood at high noon when Pablo got his men lined up. The women had prepared a quick meal, and men and women alike wolfed the grub, leaving a litter of empty cans.

Pecos approached Bass and reported the Mexicans had finished eating; then he jerked his head toward the Aleman prisoners. 'Might as well 'dobe-wall the bastards and get it over with.'

*   *   *

'I'm chicken-hearted, Pecos. Let's set 'em afoot and line 'em out. It's a fifty-mile walk, if they make it,' Bass suggested.

Pecos nodded. 'Take off your shoes, you Aleman sons of dogs! Then commence goose steppin' to to'rds Alemanda. Them as ain't outa sight in ten minutes gets shot down! Pronto!'

Ten minutes later there was no Aleman in sight. Their shoes were on the bare feet of the peons.

Pepita, dressed in her hastily-made yellow silk dress, rode up on Colonel Guzman's horse. A filled cartridge belt sagged around her slim waist, and the Luger was in its holster. Her heavy hair was braided and coiled at the nape of her neck. She was scrubbed till her skin glowed.

'These little peons need Pepa, who is a hard-boiled baby, to look after them,' she told Bass. 'You take care of Frijole Beanses for me. Some time I will settle what I have to settle with Colonel Guts. Adios, Bassito!'

Pepa herded the women on horseback and muleback, ahead of her. She waved a yellow scarf as she rode out of sight.

Pablo gave his men orders to follow him and rode off at the head of his ragtag army.

Bass watched them out of sight, then went back into the hut. The bodies of the dead Japanese and the machine gunner had been dumped in the cellar. Bass glowered at Colonel Guzman, then cut the ropes that tied him down and kicked him up on his feet.

'Get your stink outside.' Bass poked Guzman's heavy back with a gun. 'Climb aboard that mule!'

Pecos had selected a stout, rawboned mule. There was no saddle or blanket to soften the high-ridged backbone. Bass prodded the colonel's spine with the gun barrel, and the heavy-set man mounted the mule awkwardly.

When they had ridden off to a safe distance, Bass signaled to Pecos, who was on the ground alongside the detonator.

There was the dull heavy blast of the explosion. Debris was blown high, spreading into a drab-colored mushroom shape that flattened out, dissipating itself as it fell apart.

'Let's go,' Bass said, and the pack outfit got under way. 'We'll camp in the upper valley some time tonight. About sunrise tomorrow we'll make the big dicker with Butcher Guzman.'

As they rode along, Beans told Bass that Pepa's name was really Josefa Vidal, and that her brother was El Capitan Vidal.

'I wonder if Josefa knows that Pablo shot

her brother with his silver-handled gun?' Beans sounded a little worried.

'It's anybody's guess,' Bass said, wondering the same thing.

CHAPTER SIX

It was almost sundown, and Bass and his Texans were within a few miles of the upper valley where the Santa Catalina cattle were being held.

Bass and Pecos were riding in the lead of the strung-out pack train and remuda of horses. Bass focused the powerful lenses of the German-made binoculars that swung from a strap around his neck on the far ridge and reined up.

'Up on yonder ridge,' he said, 'there's a Yaqui war party of four, five hundred foot soldiers. Looks like they're fixin' to cut us off.'

Guzman had been riding directly behind Bass. Bass prodded him in the ribs with the end of his carbine barrel, and asked him, 'Them some of Butcher Guzman's soldiers, Buster?'

Those were the first words spoken to the man since they had left the jacal. The Texans had ignored him. Now and then they mentioned him in their talk, and the terms they applied to him were far from complimentary. No Texan missed his chance to show his contempt for Colonel Noel Guzman, who had been trained in the military schools of Mexico City by tutors imported from Germany, so that all the stiff-necked, ramrod-backed goose-stepping army tradition, was a part of the man who was now in his thirties.

Guzman had suffered untold humiliation at the hands of Bass and his Texans. They had poured it on and rubbed it into his hide with ridicule that had stripped him of his pride and military rank.

The colonel made a sorry sight in his soiled, sweat-marked uniform and dirty boots, sitting, awkward and miserable, astride the rawboned mule, his heavy face yellowish-gray, flabby now with fatigue. The thirty-mile ride on a barebacked mule had been a severe punishment to the man who sat a saddle poorly, but somehow he had toughed it out in stolid silence.

Prodded by the carbine barrel, Guzman straightened up. He looked at Bass with bloodshot, muddy eyes, that held all the evil vindictive hatred inside him.

Bass handed Guzman the binoculars, and he focused them on the distant foot soldiers who lined the ridge that overlooked the valley beyond. While Bass and his Texans looked on in grim amusement, Guzman straightened up slowly in an effort to sit his barebacked mule with some semblance of military bearing as he held the binoculars in grimy, hair-tufted hands. A dull color came into his sweat-streaked heavy face. His underlip thrust out as his muddy eyes, narrowing, lost their glazed look and were now ugly and crafty.

'Swinehund!' The thick guttural sound ripped from Guzman's twisted mouth. 'By Gott! Soon you will be paying for every insult, every word and every blow—for everything you have done to degrade and insult me. Hein!'

The guttural laugh that exploded from his belly bordered on maniacal hysteria. 'Five hundred Yaqui soldiers,' he said, his eyes lighting up with the hope of a condemned man whose death sentence had been suddenly reprieved. 'They stand guard under the command of a true Aleman Major. When the time comes, I myself will lead those men across the Rio Grande into Texas. Nothing will stop us. We will shoot down every Texan we find. We will put the older women to work in the fields with bullwhips. The younger ones will serve us to a better purpose.

'Texas will be Aleman Territory. The name of Texas will be changed to Alemanda. My father, General Kurt Guzman, will be emperor and dictator. No tongue but the German language shall be spoken or printed. The Japanese will have their separate colony until the United States is overthrown. Then the

Japanese will colonize California and the West Coast.'

Noel Guzman's voice shrilled hoarsely. 'Alemans! Uber Alles! That is the Aleman Plan!' He gestured wildly toward the distant soldiers camped on the ridge. Sweat trickled in thin rivulets from his bullet head with its roached bristles, down his heavy face, and body sweat darkened the tight-fitting blouse. He blinked the sweat from his inflamed eyes that stared out across the distance to the long ridge that bristled with the hired foot soldiers, who had marched down from the hills to kill men for a few centavos a day.

Bass shook his head as Pecos drew his six-shooter. The color had drained from Bass' face as he fought down the almost uncontrollable urge to kill this man as he would kill a mad dog.

Bass waited until Guzman calmed down from his outburst, watching him narrowly as the colonel's heavy breathing slowed, until the congested look ebbed, and his eyes came back into focus. It was like watching a man come slowly out from under a powerful drug. Bass waited until Guzman's bloodshot eyes looked at him before he broke the silence.

'You shore gave yourself a good time while it lasted, Buster,' Bass said tonelessly. Then turning to Pecos, he said, 'We might as well camp here till after dark, Pecos.'

Bass rolled a cigarette before he spoke

again. 'I'm takin' a couple of the boys along to work the brush of Aleman strays. Ride close herd on this sorry Uber Alles bastard. Don't lose track of the fact that he's our hole card, whenever you git the notion to kill the stinkin' thing.'

'How about me settin' up the wireless set, Bass?' Beans said. 'Lettin' Jefe Guzman know we still got his ugly son. That'll make him hold off.'

'I doubt it, Beans.' Bass shook his head. 'Give those soldiers down from the hills a gun and a handful of ca'tridges and a bottle of pulque and mebby some marijuana weed to smoke, and him no savvy the Aleman lingo. The only kind of talk a drunken soldier sabes is gun language, and you got to get in the first word. Any gringo Aleman palaver is out like Nellie's eye right now. Guzman can hold off his own Alemans. He might even keep Lobo Jones and his curly wolves from makin' a pass at us, but Jefe Guzman is just another gringo to those guys under him who takes orders from no man but Pancho Villa. That Aleman gringo Major will find that out when he wakes up some morning in hell with his throat cut.'

Bass grinned mirthlessly at the sweating Colonel who had listened to every word. Then he reined his horse, motioned for Pecos and the two rode off a ways together.

'Come dark, Pecos,' Bass said grimly, 'our best bet is to trickle through their lines into the valley where Lobo Jones and his renegades are holding the cattle. Once we're in the valley, we'll be out of range of their guns on the ridges. If Lobo Jones and his outfit puts up a scrap we'll cut 'em down without too much bother. The Aleman foot soldiers and the others on the ground, we can ride away from. Once we get into the valley, we'll start shovin' the cattle toward the Rio Grande, using Butcher Guzman's slimy son for protection.'

Bass lit his cigarette. 'Talk it over with the boys, Pecos. I'll be back around dark. I'm scoutin' out a night trail to take.'

'We'll be ready to drift when you get back, Bass,' Pecos said. 'How many men you takin' with you now?'

'I'm goin' alone,' Bass said quietly. 'A lone rider ain't so apt to be sighted.' He rode away before Pecos could put up an argument.

It was only when he had left his outfit behind him that Bass could think things out and weigh the odds. No matter how he figured it, throwing in an average good luck, the scales were tipped down, the odds far too heavy to hope for an even balance.

It had all had a fine sound while he was joshing about it, bragging and discounting odds, and he halfway believed his own careless boasting at the time. Riding out here alone, with night coming on and the enemy supper fires strung along the broken ridges, a man had to face it in cold-blooded reckoning.

Bass and his handful of Texans, for all their careless hoorahing banter, did not stand a snowball's chance in hell, and he blamed himself for getting his Texans into this tight spot.

Bass had led his border-jumpers into and out of countless tight spots, and together they had shot their way through plenty big odds, time after time. Until now there had always been a way out. They could slip across the Rio Grande into some hideout and cross back when the sign was right. They had laughed at danger, spit in the Devil's eye so many times that Bass had lost count. But this was a different deal.

The Texans were too far below the border to scatter out and cross the river by night. They were deep in enemy territory, and every man was an enemy. Even the Santa Catalina Mexicans were unfriendly, and Bass had gotten his Texans into this jackpot on account of Dona Catalina and her daughter, who had refused to get back across the Rio Grande into Texas without the whole tribe of Santa Catalina Mexicans.

So, Bass told himself, he had to make the big four-flusher play to make decoys of his Texans. Play the damned henyard hero and lead these Texans, who were his friends, the best friends a man ever had, into that suicide death-trap that lay in the valley beyond and below the long line of watch fires along the broken skyline.

Lobo Jones had ten or a dozen tough renegades to throw against each of Bass' Texans. Guzman had a hundred or two hundred Aleman foot soldiers under arms at Alemanda. There were five hundred other mercenaries waiting on the rim of the valley, and Bass was planning on taking his dozen Texans tonight into that valley and throw them into overwhelming odds.

What in the name of all hell had he been using for brains? He would be killing a dozen brave men, who were deserving of a fighting chance for their lives. This was no Alamo.

All Bass had to do right now was to turn back the few miles he had come from camp, eat supper and when dark came, travel back the way they had come. Take that same trail to Laredo that Dona Catalina and her Mexican tribe were taking. Yaqui had a hundred armed Mexicans with him. Pablo had that many peons to throw in with the Santa Catalina outfit.

Bass and his Texans had decoyed the enemy away from the Santa Catalina wagon and pack train. Dona Catalina's outfit should be starting about now, and with average luck they would be across the Rio Grande and safe in Texas by sunrise.

That same sunrise, if Bass followed the plan he had outlined to Pecos, would see Bass and his dozen Texans making their last stand in the valley of death.

All that crap he had been sending over the wireless to General Guzman, playing it like he held aces was nothing. All he had was a big, stinking slob of tallow who would get killed before he saw the next sunrise, when the enemy guns started popping.

'Big mouth Bass!' he voiced his thoughts, spitting the words into the gathering dusk, remembering that a bass was some kind of a big-mouthed fish. All the while he kept squinting into the gathering darkness ahead, calculating the distance between the scattered enemy watch-fires on the broken ridges, peering through the binoculars that brought the panorama of campfires so close that he could make out the men moving against the red glow.

Bass had come further than he had intended to come when he left the others. Darkness was closing him in from all sides, and he was in a basin with the brush high on all sides, the trail blurred out. The darkness was bringing out the campfires, and the men moving around with a sharp startling clarity as he watched through the powerful lenses.

It was as though he was within earshot and could hear the indistinct sound of the men's voices. Fascinated by the strange phenomenon, Bass kept the glasses focused on the men a quarter-mile distant, tricked for a long moment into the notion the lenses were magnifying the sound of voices as well as vision, thinking, *here is where I turn back, gather my outfit and get the hell gone while the back trail's still open. We'll cover Dona Catalina's trail. We'll flank 'em till she gets her slow-motion outfit across the river into Texas. The hell with us goin' into that suicide gun-trap set in the Aleman valley.*

Bass lowered the binoculars and the watch-fires of the enemy dimmed in the distance to focus to the naked eye, but the voices were still there. That indistinct whispering, inaudible murmur was still in focus. It was not unlike the hushed sound of bees, swarming in the darkness. It was a thousand small sounds blended into one and closing in on him like a heavy fog, coming up to block his trail, closing in on both sides and creeping up from behind.

Bass slid his six-shooter from its bolster. It was a nameless fear that sent a chill wiring along his spine. Dry leaves rustled, as if stirred by a breeze, but there was no wind in the night air. There was the snap of a dry twig, a dry branch broken off in another direction. Dense underbrush whispered like a big snake crawling on the ground in his direction.

Bass could feel the big palomino horse hunch and quiver under him, head up, ears twitching, whistling now through flared nostrils. He knew the animal was ready to spook, but too well-trained to lunge and whirl. Bass felt the same panic himself as he gripped his gun, eyes straining into the black shadows.

There was nothing there to shoot at, however.

The yapping of a coyote shattered the other indistinct sounds. Another joined in, then another and another, each in a different pitch. It was like a hundred, a thousand coyotes blended into a crazy chorus. There is something about a coyote's yapping that has a mad, insane cadence, as if the animal was snapping, tearing, ripping anything within reach of its white-fanged jaws. Two coyotes can make the confused racket of a whole pack.

A coyote is a sneaking, cowardly, cunning, treacherous animal when alone, but running in packs, they can hamstring a big steer, dragging it down from behind, to bite chunks from under the animal's tail. They can snapbite the inner rump while the wounded steer dies a slow-torture death. The coyotes rip, tear, and slice raw chunks till the steer's entrails spill, snapping at each other in their greed, keeping up their crazy, rabied yapping chorus.

Bass had been listening to coyotes and lobo wolves since babyhood. He had heard tales of small packs of rabied coyotes that traveled until they killed one another. Stockmen had spread the rabies among the coyotes, hoping by that means to exterminate them. He recalled it now as he gripped his gun, the wild yapping dinning in the ears like a hundred coyotes closing in on a man a-horseback. Knowing now, as more coyote yips joined the crazy chorus, that these were two-legged coyotes, that he had ridden into the broad middle of a bunch of drunken soldiers having their fun as they closed in for the kill.

The big palomino was terrified now, trembling and whistling through flared nostrils. Bass knew that the soldiers were probably wearing coyote pelts, smeared with the dread scent of the animal. He had all he could manage to keep his seat in the saddle as his horse whirled and lunged into the thorny brush. Mesquite and cat-claw limbs raked his face.

Bass pulled both feet from the stirrups as the horse reared up and came over backward, throwing himself free. He tried to land on his feet, stumbled and fell. Using all the skill of long years of horsemanship, he tried to roll clear of the shod hooves. The crazy yapping ceased as abruptly as it had begun, in that split-second before his head exploded in a black, soundless crash.

Bass lay like a man dead, sprawled there on his back, the sluggish blood oozing from his ripped scalp where a shod hoof had struck a glancing blow.

The big palomino was on its feet now, stampeding in its terror along the back trail, the heavy tapadero-covered stirrups swinging and slapping against the horse's ribs.

While a score of soldiers in cotton pants and shirts, moved from the brush on all sides, their eyes glittering as they grouped around the

Texan who lay without moving on the ground. They were jabbering and laughing at the joke they had played as they unfastened the tanned coyote pelts from their heads. All were naked to the waist, their skins slick with the vile-smelling grease they had smeared on, the sweat beading their faces and bodies. Standing grouped, they tilted their heads skyward and the crazy yelping coyote chorus dinned and echoed into the night, to carry up the broken slope to the other soldiers grouped around the watch-fires, to voice the message of their kill.

None of the soldiers had guns, but each and every man had a heavy-bladed machete in his belt or gripped in a grease-smeared hand.

The coyote yapping ended abruptly. When the last echoes had died away, they picked up Bass' limp body and carried it up the rough, broken slope of the ridge.

*　　*　　*

Bass squinted his eyes tight shut before the dazzling flame burned his eyeballs out and set fire to the inside of his skull. He was tied down hand and foot beside a scorching fire while he twisted, squirmed, grit his teeth and suffered the agonies of hell until his strength was spent. The sonsabitches were roasting him alive. He lay there, waiting, hoping that this was some damnable nightmare, but knowing full well that he was awake and alive and being tortured.

It took an effort to pry his lids open under the blinding heat glare.

'You owe me twenty-five head of good mules.' El Lobo's voice was like a crosscut saw being sharpened with a dull file. 'One hundred carbines, one hundred rounds of ammunition for each gun.'

Bass slivered his eyes open as El Lobo smashed the end of the beer bottle against his spurred bootheel. His pale eyes looked colorless as he skinned back his upper lip to show big yellow-stained teeth.

'No Texan sonofabitch can die off, owin' me that much.' Jones scratched Bass' naked belly with the sharp, jagged end of the broken bottle and watched the green bottleflies swarming on the thin line of blood that filled the deep scratch marks.

'Them damned green bottleflies,' Lobo Jones chuckled. 'I like to watch 'em fill up and dump their screw worm eggs that'll hatch out before sundown. It's the damnedest thing, the way Nature gits the job done. There's half a dozen bottleflies on you, layin' maggot eggs right now. Soon as they think they got it all to theirselves,' he said, his pale eyes squinting as his grin widened, 'I'll have the men move you over to one of them big ant hills.

'That's where the fun actually commences,' Jones leered. 'The red ants doin' battle with the screw worms. Puncture a man's eardrums.

Them screw worms git through to the brain in no time. That's when you go plumb crazy locoed before you die off.'

El Lobo sat back on his bootheels, the bottle of tequila in his hand, the wolfish grin on his face.

'Open your jaws, Bass, and I'll give you a drink to keep you happy, or I kin knock your teeth out with a gun barrel and pour in the rotgut that keeps you alive. You ain't in no shape to git choosy, you Texan sonofabitch.'

Bass opened his jaws and swallowed the raw tequila. He had to keep swallowing fast or choke to death.

Lobo Jones sat the empty bottle on Bass' chest, balancing it there. 'Providin' General Guzman kicks through with the bounty he's been offerin' on your hide,' El Lobo said as he took a thick cigarette rolled in black paper from his pocket and lit it, 'I'll break better than even on that pack train you hijacked, so far as the dinero is concerned.' He sucked the smoke deep into his lungs and leaned over to blow it into Bass' face. 'But Butcher Guzman is a crooked bastard.

'I'm playin' this trick on you just for the hell of it.' He shoved his scarred fist into Bass' face. 'And to pay for this little souvenir you once gave me. The leaders are cut in my thumb and two fingers.' He shoved the flat of his hand into Bass' face.

'Show you I'm kind hearted, Bass. I'm givin'

you butts on this marijuana reefer. Clamp down on it before it drops into your mouth, and the hot coal burns your tonsils.'

'Was machts du, Herr Wolff?' asked a skinny man in an Aleman uniform, who had come up to stand across Bass' spread-eagled body. The man's bony, gray face, the same dirty gray as the uniform, had the look of a death mask. From this skull-like face showed a pair of glittering eyes that had no color. The head under the red cap that he took off, was bald and shiny with sweat, the transparent skin stretched tight to show the color of the skull bone.

'I'm keepin' this Texican alive, Major, so that he kin answer Jefe Guzman's questions when the big dog with the brass stars gits here. The Jefe wants to find out what this Texican bastard did to his boy Noel.'

'You are drunk, Herr Wolff.' The colorless eyes in the death mask glittered.

'Hell, yes.' El Lobo got to his feet, hitching up the two crossed cartridge belts that sagged across his heavy flanks. 'I'm goin' to git a hell of a lot drunker. You kin save your orders for your Aleman goose-steppers. To hell with that Herr Wolff crap. El Lobo don't salute nobody, Baldy.'

Bass lay there helpless, harmless, harmless as a hog-tied bull. He spat the marijuana cigarette out as he watched the two men stand there, glaring into each other's eyes, their hands on their guns.

The raw tequila had set fire to Bass' belly and guts, and red pain throbbed inside his head. He wondered how soon Butcher Guzman would be here. It was long past sunrise now. Bass wondered what had become of Pecos and his Texans, Beans and his wireless outfit—and the prisoner, Colonel Noel Guzman, Bass' ace in, the hole. Dona Catalina should be in Texas now.

Bass heard the pounding of shod hooves and the creak of saddle leather, the jingle of spurs.

A Mexican, riding a palomino horse, came up. He was a short, heavy-set paunchy man in a flat-brimmed Stetson hat, a brush-scarred charro jacket and bullhide chaps. His face was covered by black whiskers. White teeth, bared in a pulled-back grin, left his black eyes cold. The paunchy man was forking the palomino Bass had ridden last evening into the coyote trap.

A dozen heavily armed, well-mounted Mexicans had come up with him, reining their blowing, sweat-wet horses to a sliding halt behind their leader.

'Who's this hombre you have staked out on the ground?' the Mexican demanded. 'And who are you?'

'A Texican renegade called Bass Slocum.' Lobo Jones thumbed back his hat. 'I'm called El Lobo. I am with General Guzman's Aleman

Army. Who the hell wants to know?'

'Colonel Baca.' The white teeth showed suddenly again in the black-whiskered face. 'With Pancho Villa's Army.' He laid a pair of thick-muscled hands on the saddle horn, leaning a little forward, his hat slanted across his hard, black eyes. 'That's who the hell wants to know.'

Baca shoved back his hat, mocking the gesture of Lobo Jones. Without taking his hard stare from the tall, tow-headed renegade, he barked an order at the dozen armed Mexicans who had ridden up with him.

'Behold here,' the Villista Colonel said, his voice heavy in its mockery, 'the one who calls himself El Lobo. He has a lobo wolf pack for a following. They are holding the Santa Catalina cattle below in the valley. Six of you go along to see to it that this El Lobo hombre gets back where he belongs with the cattle. If he hesitates, shoot him in the back. Bring back the guns and horse and saddle.

'My Yaquis have been told to keep you and your pack of mangy wolves in the valley, to kill you if you try to sneak out,' Baca continued. 'Those orders come from Pancho Villa. Get on your horse and vamos. Get the hell out of my eyes!' A six-shooter showed in one brown hand, the gun pointed at Lobo Jones' belly.

The tall, towheaded renegade's sun-reddened face whitened. He was no man's coward if he had the bulge, but he read the look in the Villista's hard black eyes. He did his best to put a swagger into his walk as he headed for his horse, but with a dozen guns pointed carelessly in his direction, his style was cramped.

CHAPTER SEVEN

The Villista colonel had shoved his six-shooter back into its carved holster. He had a thin corn husk in one hand, and he was taking black tobacco from his pocket, spilling it into the corn husk, spreading it with a stubby forefinger, then rolling the cigarette into shape, twisting one end in to hold the tobacco, and gripping it between his thumb and fingers. He lit it from the match flame cupped in his other hand. His beady, black stare now fixed on the tall Aleman Major with the skull face, paying no further attention to Lobo Jones who mounted and rode away, followed by half a dozen of the Mexicans with naked carbines.

'Now, Senor, we'll pay attention to you,' Baca said. The thick smoke coming through the wide nostrils screened the words. 'And what in hell is your business up here?'

The Aleman skeleton in the red-trimmed gray uniform brought the heels of his high black boots together as he stood ramrod stiff. 'I am an Aleman Major, sent here to take charge of the Yaqui recruits, to drill and train these men.'

Twin jets of tobacco smoke spurted from the splayed nostrils of the Villista Colonel, as he snorted. 'Diablo! Colonel Baca of the Villista Army is in command of these men. I have heard about the goose-trot drill. It is lucky I get here in time before these soldiers kill you complete.

'You will depart now, muy pronto. You will tell General Guzman to deliver pronto, at once, the rifles and cartridges he was supposed to have here for my men. If they don't get the rifles and bullets and the pay in advance, they go back to their hills. Give that message to General Guzman from Colonel Baca, who speaks for Pancho Villa. Now get the hell out of my eyes!' He made a quick gesture.

'See that the Aleman goose-stepper leaves for Alemanda muy pronto.' He told six of his Mexicans to go along.

When the Aleman Major had gone, followed by his armed escort, the Villista Colonel rubbed out the stub of his corn husk cigarette against his bullhide chaps. He lifted his voice, barking his commands in the Yaqui tongue.

Bass caught the glint of knives as the rawhide thongs were severed to set him free and the taste of water in his mouth, the splashing of water as one bucketful after another was poured all over his naked body, until he was drenched and sopping. He felt himself being lifted and carried, all the while only partly conscious and half-aware of what was happening to him.

He had been staked out for so long that there was no feeling in his arms or legs. He was only aware of the dull pain that throbbed inside his skull. Then they were rubbing the blood back into his arms and legs, and a million hot needles were stinging into his fingertips and toes, into his hands and feet and upward. After a time the needling pain was gone, and whoever it was who had been working on him left and the voices had receded into the distance and were no more.

Bass was inside a tent, lying on a canvas cot. The Villista Colonel, a short, stocky man, in a pair of old chaps that were saddle-warped to the shape of his short, bowed legs, was standing in the doorway of the tent. His hard paunch sagged over the belt of his chaps. His flat-crowned Stetson hat was shoved back from a shock of coarse black hair. His sharp eyes were watching Bass from under heavy brows that tufted above a splayed nose. He had a bottle in his hand and was digging the cork out with a knife blade.

'It's time to rise and shine, Tejano. There is water to drink in the bucket. Rench the bad taste and spit it out—to enjoy the taste of good tequila.'

Bass washed the dirty taste from his mouth

and drank from the battered tin dipper.

'Drink slow, or you puke it back.' The Villista shoved the remnants of the cork into the bottle with the long knife blade, and handed Bass the bottle.

Bass lifted the bottle. 'Salud!' he croaked, and took a couple of big swallows of the raw tequila.

'Muy gracias,' Bass forced a slow grin. 'Thanks for everything.'

'Por nada.' The Villista shrugged thick shoulders and lifted the bottle. 'Put on your clothes. They are there beside you.' The white teeth showed as he lifted the bottle.

Bass put on his clothes and pulled on his boots. He put his hat on slowly over the scalp wound.

The Villista Colonel tossed the bulging saddlebags from Bass' saddle on the cot alongside where he sat. 'It is filled with papers, Tejano.' Baca's eyes glittered wickedly. 'I am an ignorant Mexican with some Yaqui blood in my veins. I have never learned to read or write. I put a mark for the name I have. I am ignorant like Pancho Villa. I am always superstitious about the written papers.' He commenced rolling a corn husk cigarette. 'Explain the papers you carry with you in the saddle pockets, Tejano,' he said, his voice harsh.

Bass unbuckled the straps. He took out the bloodstained Aleman flag that he had stuffed in on top of the propaganda pamphlets.

'That's the Aleman flag,' Bass said grimly. 'The red and yellow Villista colors. The red ball of the Japanese. The black cross of the Alemans here in Mexico. These papers concern the big Aleman Plan,' Bass told him in a voice that had a gritty sound. 'You have perhaps heard of this Guzman Aleman Plan?'

'No. I have been back in the hills, rounding up men to fight for Pancho Villa. I was told that this General Guzman would have the money to pay them for fighting. Jefe Guzman has plenty rifles and ammunition. I saw many foot soldiers wearing gray uniforms with the red strip and the red caps, marching back and forth, like locoed horses that step high, I was told this was the Aleman goose-walk and those were Aleman soldiers come to fight for Pancho Villa.' The brown hands made a gesture. 'What is this, the Guzman Aleman Plan, Tejano?'

Bass got out one of the pamphlets. He read it to the Villista, and he explained the Aleman Plan in detail.

'Guzman would take all of Texas,' Bass said. 'He would kill off all the men, put the older women in the fields to work, the young girls in houses, to be sold for a night to any man who had the price. Guzman would use Texas for a breeding ground for his Aleman tribe. When there were enough Alemans, they would overthrow the United States Government, using Mexican soldiers. After they had taken the United States, they would take Mexico, killing all the men, treating the women according to the Aleman Plan.'

Bass rapped the bulging saddlebags. 'It is there in the papers I found at the Aleman wireless station.

'I took Jefe Guzman's son, Colonel Noel Guzman, a prisoner,' Bass continued. 'He was still with my Texans when I left them last night before dark. I was scouting alone for a way into the valley when your men played their coyote game on me, and I woke up, staked out like you found me.'

'My men have no guns,' Colonel Baca said. 'Only knives and machetes. They have orders to let no man come into the valley. You and your Tejanos were coming after the cattle claimed by Jefe Guzman, no?'

'To trail the cattle into Texas for Dona Catalina,' said Bass. 'The cattle are in the Santa Catalina brand.'

'What of that El Lobo and his wolf pack?'

'We were to wipe 'em out,' said Bass, 'if they put up any kind of a fight.'

'Jefe Guzman and his goose-walk foot soldiers? What about them?'

'A Texan on horseback shouldn't have too much trouble dodgin' foot soldiers.'

The Villista showed his teeth. 'Pancho Villa promised the Santa Catalina Grant, and all the livestock, to Jefe Guzman as a reward for furnishing guns and cartridges to my men when I fetched them down from their stronghold in the hills.' The Colonel scowled thoughtfully. 'But this Aleman Plan could make Pancho Villa change his mind,' he conceded. 'Villa doesn't know anything about this, I assure you. Nor would he like it.

'I sent word to Jefe Guzman to come here.' The Villista held the bottle in both hands in a grip that made the brown knuckles turn bone-white. 'I shall ask this Jefe Guzman concerning these papers, question him closely in regard to the Aleman Plan.' The black eyes looked in Bass' hard, gray eyes. 'I hope for your sake, Tejano, that you have not lied to me.'

'Maybe Jefe Guzman will do the lyin'. If you can't read what's printed here, you have no way of knowing which one of us is telling the truth.'

'I will have a Mexican here who will read what you have read to me, when the time comes.' The white teeth showed as the Villista handed Bass the bottle.

'I am anxious concerning my men,' Bass said, holding the bottle.

'Your Tejanos have been notified concerning your capture. They have been warned, likewise, to stay out of the valley. Your Tejanos have been told to camp where they are. That is good tequila. Drink it and pass the bottle; too much talk dries the throat, Tejano.'

Bass watched the Villista Colonel buckle

down the straps to close the flaps on the bulging saddlebags. He looked at the silk flag, as if admiring the startling colors, scowling at the bloodstains. When he looked up, Bass answered the question in his opaque eyes.

'I crippled the Japanese fellow that ran the wireless station. He ran a long bladed hari-kari knife up under his brisket into his gizzard. He had the flag around his belly. That's how it got bloodstained.'

The Villista shoved the flag into the pocket of his chaps. 'I think maybe Pancho Villa will like a look at this flag.' He hung the saddlebags over a rawhide kyack, slapping the leather with the flat of his hand. 'Also what's in this saddle pockets, what you call the Aleman Plan.'

Bass knew and understood the Villista and his breed of man. He had grown up amongst them, gone to grade school with them at Laredo. Even below the border he had felt at home amongst them. He had eaten with them, shared a bottle and tobacco. He had always been welcome at their bailes. This was the first time he had ever been thought of as an enemy of the people of Mexico. He was a prisoner now, instead of a welcome guest. Bass had always been simpatico, and it gave him a strange feeling inside. It must have shown in his eyes because the Villista Colonel was the first to look away.

Bass' old chaps, together with his cartridge

belt and holstered gun, were in a far corner of the army tent. The Villista walked over and picked up the chaps. He dug a hand into the pocket and pulled out an unopened sack of Bull Durham and a book of wheatstraw papers. He handed the cigarette makings to Bass.

Bass shook his head. 'I couldn't keep it down.' He rolled a cigarette and lit it. The tobacco smoke tasted good. 'A man feels plumb naked without a gun,' he volunteered.

'There is a revolution inside of Mexico.' Baca's words had a harsh brutal sound. 'We're not playing games.' The Villista took Bass' gun from its holster and shoved it into the pocket of his own chaps, along with the silk flag. 'The de la Guerra family is Federalista. You are working for Dona Catalina. You and your Tejanos would get her cattle shoved across the Rio Grande into Texas, when all the Santa Catalina cattle, horses and mules have been confiscated and belong to the Villistas. You are a prisoner. Before tomorrow your Tejanos may be prisoners, or dead perhaps. Quien sabe?

'You had your chance, Tejano. Pancho Villa sent you word that if Bass Slocum and his Tejanos wished to join the Villistas, they would be well-rewarded, but you refused the offer. You hijacked a pack train and took a hundred guns and ammunition. Those guns were por me, hombre. Por Colonel Baca and his men.

Por Dios, hombre! Now you want your gun given back!' He jerked open the tent flap, throwing it back. He pointed a blunt thumb backward as he faced Bass, who was on his feet now.

'Behold who comes, Tejano.' Baca's eyes glittered. 'General Kurt Guzman, Jefe of Alemanda. Take notice of the special Aleman soldier escort.'

Bass' bloodshot gray eyes narrowed as he watched Jefe Guzman and the skull-head Aleman Major ride into sight. They rode about twenty feet in the lead of their military escort. Bass went cold and a little sick when he recognized Pablo, the Santa Catalina Major Domo, riding in the lead of the same Mexican Aleman recruits that he had sent to join Dona Catalina's cavalcade.

'Keep your tongue behind your teeth,' the Villista Colonel growled. 'Your life and the lives of your Tejanos depend on your actions. I put no trust in that Jefe Guzman. That Pablo is a traitor and therefore not to be trusted.' He yanked the tent flap down. He picked up Bass' cartridge belt and empty holster and tossed it to him.

Bass buckled on the belt. He watched the Villista shove his six-shooter deep into one of the saddle pockets and put the Aleman silk flag in to cover the gun. 'So you know where to find your gun, Tejano. Soon will come the showdown inside this tent. My men have no guns, no bullets. I have only these dozen Mexican Villistas who will be somewhere around. Jefe Guzman has the traitor Pablo and about a hundred peon Alemans, all with guns. Besides, consider El Lobo and his wolf pack, who are ready to back whatever move Jefe Guzman will make.' The Villista picked up the half-emptied bottle and held it in his thick hand.

'I am giving you a second chance to join the Villistas. You and your Tejanos,' he said.

'I'm your huckleberry,' Bass answered.

'Is no better than a fighting chance.'

'It beats no chance at all. If I had my men here, it would cut down the odds,' Bass said grimly.

'Your Tejanos are on their way. You join the Villistas right now?'

'Hell, yes.'

'Viva Villa!' The white teeth showed. 'Salud!' He took a big drink and handed the bottle to Bass.

'Viva Villa!' said Bass quietly. 'Salud!'

The Villista banded Bass the saddlebags. 'Aviso! Remember this. Keep your tongue behind your teeth, Tejano. Sit down and act like a prisoner of war.'

Bass nodded grimly. 'You got the deal, Colonel. I'll play 'em as you toss 'em my way.'

''Sta bueno, compadre.' The Villista stepped outside, dropping the tent flap to leave Bass alone inside.

'Senores!' There was a grim mockery in Baca's salutation, the heavy tone of his voice, the white-toothed grin, the glinting opaque black of his eyes that flicked the naked carbine barrels of Pablo's uniformed peons lined up behind the paunchy Jefe and the Aleman Major.

'You are a brave man indeed, Senor Guzman.' The Villista Colonel ignored the drawn carbines, ignored the threatening scowl on Guzman's face as he gripped the Luger in his belted holster.

'Either that,' Colonel Baca continued, as his thick fingers twisted a husk cigarette into shape, 'or you put as cheap a value on your own life as you do on the lives of those hombres who are in your disfavor.' He pulled a kitchen match across the butt of one of the pair of holstered guns and held the cupped flame to his cigarette.

'Those peons with you, Senor,' Baca said, flicking the burning match stick through the air, 'are not yet accustomed to the use of the guns they hold. Por Dios, Senor, if that Pablo game rooster was to give the command to fire, some of the lead bullets would go into your back, Senor.' The smoke spurted from the Villista's splayed nostrils.

'I compliment you, Senor,' he went on, 'on your faith in those men you have dressed up in strange uniforms. Your broad back makes an excellent target. You would, perhaps, feel safer on the ground, facing the guns, as I stand.'

Baca let out a sharp barking laugh. 'Besides that, what are they afraid of that they must wave the guns around. This is a Villista camp.' He made a gesture with the half-smoked cigarette.

As if it had been some pre-arranged signal, the Villista's men appeared as if by some conjuror's trick. In bunches of half a dozen, they rose to their feet from behind every clump of brush and from behind each boulder. Tall men for the most part, lean and wiry of stature, the black eyes glinting from faces that looked crudely carved from the native mahogany. Their faded cotton shirts and pants and the huaraches and straw sombreros had a uniform sameness. A rawhide thong held up the cotton pants. Their only weapons were heavy-bladed, wicked-looking machetes. In a matter of seconds they surrounded Jefe Guzman, the Aleman Major and Pablo's armed escort.

CHAPTER EIGHT

The Villista Colonel held the cigarette to his whiskered mouth, the red coal burning the dry husk that held the black tobacco as he sucked the smoke into his lungs and snorted it out through his nostrils, while he watched the sweat break out through the coarse pores of the Jefe's oily skin as Guzman shifted uneasily in his cavalry saddle.

Colonel Baca paid no attention to the skull-faced Aleman Major. The black eyes cut a quick look at Pablo, who was uncomfortable, sullen-eyed, defiant, as if he dreaded whatever was to come.

'You can perceive with your own eyes, Senor,' Colonel Baca said as he stubbed the coal of the smoked-down cigarette on his bullhide chaps. 'My men are unarmed. They need the guns you promised Pancho Villa.' He hitched up his sagging cartridge belts. 'Besides the guns and the bullets, Senor, there is a matter of pay. These men want the pay in advance. They know the meaning of a peso when it is laid on the ground for them to pick up.'

Baca hooked both thumbs in the heavy cartridge belts. 'I told these Yaquis back in the hills certain things that concern Jefe Guzman, the big politico, pertaining to the great wealth, muy rico, muy opulento, like the king, the big dog with the brass collars. Such a muy grande Senor keeps his promise, even to the peon. Surely such a man of high honor keeps his word to these men, concerning the guns and the bullets and the pesos laid on the line.'

The Villista Colonel shrugged his shoulders. 'Behold these men, Senor. Take notice of the sad disappointment on their faces. They wait like children. They perceive the guns in the hands of peons who are accustomed to shovels and hoes in the fields. I read it in their eyes how they would be eager to snatch away the guns from those clumsy hands. My men are familiar with guns, Senor. It would be wise to humor their eager desires in these matters. Perhaps the guns and the bullets and the pesos are on the way here? It would give me great pleasure to so advise my men, Senor.'

Bass had been watching through a narrow slit in the tent flap, one hand inside the saddlebags across his arm. The feel of the gun was reassuring.

Bass could see the sweat running down the heavy, brutal, pockmarked face of Jefe Guzman. The General's gray blouse was dark stained with it. There was pure hatred in his muddy eyes as they swiveled in heavy pouches. Jefe Guzman, despite his disadvantage, was a hard man to bluff.

'Pah!' Guzman spat it out, the thick spittle spraying the air. 'I have no speech to make to these pelados. The rifles and ammunition are at the arsenal at Alemanda. They earn their fighting pay before they get so much as a centavo. I have no time to waste making speeches to this pelado scum.'

Guzman swung down heavily to the ground, his high black boots puffing the dust. He barked a sharp guttural command in German to the skull-faced Aleman Major, who dismounted stiffly to stand alongside the paunchy Jefe.

The lean and the fat of it, Bass grinned to himself, as Jefe Guzman gave orders to Pablo.

'When I enter the tent with this man,' the General said, 'you will have your men surround it. Let nobody enter until I give the command.'

He swung around heavily to glare at the Villista Colonel. 'Send those ignorant pelados away somewhere out of sight. They'll get their guns and ammunition and their bellies full of fighting before long. They'll be paid if their job is satisfactory. Right now, there are things I must discuss in private with you. What have you to offer in the way of refreshments?' he asked, pulling the gray tunic down across his paunch.

'I can only offer you the Indio pulque,' Colonel Baca said sarcastically. 'There is little here to offer the muy rico Jefe Guzman, whose saloons and cantinas have the finest of liquor to offer to great politicos, such as yourself, Senor.'

'You drink your pulque. I'll drink the schnapps we fetched along.' Guzman cleared his throat and spat in the dirt. 'You are holding a prisoner, a Tejano bandit by the name of Bass Slocum. I want the prisoner fetched to me without delay.'

'I have forseen your anticipation pertaining to that matter, Senor.'

Bass stepped back, his hand still gripping the gun inside the saddle pocket, as the Villista Colonel threw back the tent flap.

Jefe Guzman had stalked into the middle of the tent before he caught sight of Bass, who was standing to one side of him.

'Take 'er easy, Mister,' Bass said in a cold voice.

The Villista jabbed a thumb in the lean back of the Aleman Major, who thought it was a gun against his spine, as he entered the tent in a couple of stiff-legged strides.

'Stick around, Pablo,' Colonel Baca called back across his shoulder. 'We'll call you inside when it comes your turn.' He dropped the flap into place.

'It's better to leave the guns where they belong, Senores. The sound of any shooting might get the men excited.'

Bass eyed Jefe Guzman as if seeing him for the first time. The color had drained from Guzman's swarthy face to leave it a sickly, yellowish hue. The muddy eyes had a glazed look as he stared at Bass, his mouth open, his heavy jaw slacked on his double chin. Then hate filled the eyes, and the heavy jaws snapped shut.

It was the Villista Colonel who answered the question in Guzman's eyes.

'The Tejanos are still holding Noel Guzman a prisoner, Senor. So far no harm has befallen your son. So far, so good, no? Perhaps his future health depends upon the outcome of this meeting.' He made a sweeping gesture. 'Be seated, Senores. The camp stools are the best I have to offer.'

Colonel Baca fished a sealed bottle of aged yellow tequila from a rawhide kyack. The blade of his knife glinted as it gouged out the cork.

The Aleman Major was pulling the cork on a quart bottle of kummel with a corkscrew, the handle of which telescoped into a silver cup. He filled the cup to the brim and handed it to the Jefe, who downed the drink at a gulp, then reached for the bottle. He downed three drinks while the Villista was knifing the stubborn bits of cork from the neck of the tequila bottle.

Jefe Guzman stood there with the square bottle in one hand, the silver cup in the other. The matched pair of heavy gold rings with the oversized, over-ripe, red rubies, that he wore on the third finger of each fat hand, had an obscene glitter. He belched loudly, spat on the dirt floor of the tent, then his thick underlip thrust out, and his eyes grew crafty and cruel.

'You want guns and ammunition and pay in advance for your men.' Guzman's voice was heavy with hatred and contempt. He gestured at Bass with the bottle. 'But for this hombre, this blundering Texican, the guns and ammunition would have been here last night. My son, Noel, would have delivered them.

Fetch my son here, and I will instruct him to guide your men to the arsenal and deliver them the guns and ammunition. The pesos will have to wait until later.' Guzman filled the cup and drank.

'That can be arranged, Senor.' The Villista's eyes glittered. 'Muy pronto.'

'I demand that this Texican be delivered as a prisoner to me. Pablo and his peon Aleman recruits will take Bass Slocum to the carcel at Alemanda to stand trial.'

'That likewise can easily be arranged, Senor,' Colonel Baca agreed.

The Villista shoved the opened bottle at Bass, and as Bass grabbed it, the Colonel yanked the pair of saddle pockets from his arm, backing away quickly. Bass made no effort to grab the saddle pocket where the Villista had put his six-shooter. Bass had already transferred the gun. It was inside his shirt now, shoved into the waistband of his levis. He met the look in the black eyes with a mirthless grin.

'Al momento, Senor.' The Villista unbuckled a strap on the saddle pocket and brought out the silk flag and spread it out on the table. Then he tossed one of the pamphlets alongside the flag.

'These things have been brought to my attention, Senor.' He buckled the strap and tossed the saddlebags back to Bass, who made a swift catch.

'You have time to explain what the so-ignorant pelado, Colonel Baca, has not sufficient brains to comprehend, while we await the arrival of your son.'

Colonel Baca pulled back the tent flap, the hard black eyes cutting Bass a swift look of warning.

Bass saw Pablo sitting his horse in front of the tent. He saw the sullen look in Pablo's eyes as the traitor caught sight of Bass. Then Bass noted something he had not observed before. The Mexicans in the crinkled, dirty-gray Aleman uniforms and red caps were not the ones who had escorted Jefe Guzman. He recognized half a dozen faces that belonged to the Santa Catalina Mexicans.

The Villista Colonel barked out some order in the Yaqui tongue. One of the men in the gray uniform gave answer. Even before Bass caught sight of the man, he recognized the voice. It belonged to the giant Yaqui of the Santa Catalina Rancho. It was no more than a brief glimpse that Bass caught of Yaqui, who looked ridiculous in the Aleman uniform that was far too small, before he reined his horse and was gone. The tentflap dropped. Bass caught the glint of warning in the black eyes as they flicked him.

'Your son will be here without further delay, Senor.' The Villista picked up the pamphlet. 'I am an ignorant pelado, who has never learned to read, Senor. This Tejano has read what is printed here, so I have no more than his word for what he calls the Guzman Aleman Plan.' The white teeth showed. 'Perhaps, Senor, we should have Pablo read what is written here, no? Before I send it by messenger to Pancho Villa.'

'Pancho Villa,' Jefe Guzman said, 'is fully informed concerning the great Aleman Plan and is in full agreement with its details.' He pulled the tent flap aside.

'Dismount, Pablo. Come inside,' Baca called.

Pablo's eyes were sullen, suspicious, as he came into the tent. His attempt at a swagger was a pitiful failure. Pablo had the look of a trapped animal.

'Read what is written here, Pablo.' Colonel Baca shoved the pamphlet at him. 'Por favor.'

Pablo's eyes took on a look of wary defiance. 'One should know what has gone on,' he said, his hand on his silver-handled gun, 'and what is occurring now. I do not trust in this Tejano who is supposed to be a prisoner. Por Dios, his are not the actions that become a man who is to be shot at sundown.' He tossed the pamphlet back on the table.

'You suspect treachery of some sort?' Guzman's eyes narrowed.

The Villista shoved the bottle of tequila at Pablo, who took it in his left hand. 'Perhaps the traitor from the Santa Catalina Rancho cannot read and takes this attitude to save his pride. Let the tequila put warmth into your guts for what is yet to come, hombre.

'You are to accompany this Tejano prisoner to the carcel at Alemanda, where he will stand kangaroo court trial and be condemned without delay to be stood with his back to the adobe wall of the carcel, and be shot down by a firing squad. Por Dios, this prisoner is but showing the boasted courage of the Tejano. Bass Slocum is free under the rules of Ley del Fuego, to be shot down if he attempts to escape. Behold the empty holster where the gun should be. Put tequila into your guts, hombre!'

Every man inside the tent stiffened at the sudden confusion of scuffling sounds outside. Then the thick voice of Noel Guzman came grating through.

'Gott in Himmel! You would shove me into a trap to be shot down!'

Jefe Guzman let out a guttural cry as he threw aside the tent flap. Noel staggered inside, and his father threw both arms around his son. The disheveled Noel returned the embrace with a limp response.

Bass cut a look at the tall Aleman Major. He saw the contempt and disgust in the skull face and pale eyes before the Aleman wiped it away with a skeleton hand.

Then Bass sighted a quick glimpse of the giant Yaqui outside, who was holding up a Luger for Bass to see. Then Yaqui stepped back and was lost to sight. The Villista Colonel dropped the tent flap.

'Keep your tongue behind your teeth.' The Villista hissed the warning in Bass' ear. 'Keep the shirt on, Tejano.'

Somebody had given Jefe Guzman's son a working over, so recently that the blood had not had time to dry. Noel Guzman had the look of a man who had tried to tame a wildcat. He looked clawed, rather than beaten, and the claw marks had raked both cheeks. His eyes looked gouged and were swelling shut, puffy and discolored where fists had battered. Even the thick, oily hair looked like it had been torn loose from the grimy scalp.

'Instruct your son, Senor,' the Villista said, his thumbs hooked in the sagging cartridge belts, so that both hands were within reach of his two guns, 'regarding the terms of the agreement Colonel Baca of the Villista Army had fulfilled his end of the bargain. Time is running short for General Kurt Guzman, Jefe of Alemanda, to prove that the Senor is a man of honor, who keeps his promises. It is time for Colonel Noel Guzman to take my men to their guns and bullets. It is not advisable to try the patience of those men.'

Jefe Guzman was scowling darkly. He started to speak in the German language to his son.

'Talk in the Mexican tongue,' the Villista said sharply. 'Better yet, I, myself, will instruct

Colonel Noel Guzman, that he may fully understand with the complete comprehension.' He thrust himself between the paunchy Jefe and his disheveled son.

'It is understood, Senor Noel Guzman,' Baca said, 'that you are to take my men to the arsenal near Alemanda and deliver to them the guns and bullets promised them by your most generous father. You will accompany them on their return here, where your father will be waiting your prompt return.

'It is further agreed that the Tejano, Bass Slocum, will accompany Pablo as a prisoner, to the carcel at Alemanda. That is about to be done promptly, without delay.' He motioned with a jerk of his head.

'Pablo, take charge of the Tejano prisoner. Take care that you deliver him alive to the carcel. In the event of failure, your punishment will be severe. There is no need to tie the hands of the prisoner. He is under Ley del Puego. If he is so foolish as to attempt to escape, shoot to cripple him only. Under no circumstances is the Tejano to be killed.'

Colonel Baca reached into a kyack and pulled out a bottle of tequila. He handed it to Bass. 'Adios, Tejano. Meet death with bravery as becomes a Texan. Put the bottle in the saddle bags, to warm your gizzard.' He threw back the tent flap, and Bass stepped outside.

Taking Colonel Guzman by the arm that he managed to twist up behind his back in a hammerlock, the Villista propelled him outside into the hands of the giant Yaqui from the Santa Catalina Grant.

Back inside the tent, the Villista closed the flap. His hands were on his guns as he spoke to Jefe Guzman. 'I have military duties that need my attention, Senor. You and your Aleman Major will use my pelado quarters as your own until your son returns, but if you grow impatient in your desire to reach Alemanda, there will be no barrier to block the return trail. Adios, Major death-warmed over. I salute General Guzman, Jefe of Alemanda.' Colonel Baca backed out of the tent.

'Hold on!' Jefe Guzman shoved his big paunch through the tent flap. 'I must speak to my son before he leaves.'

'He is already on his way, Senor. Your son will return in the same condition in which he departed.'

'What kind of trick is this?'

Colonel Baca's brown hands were on his guns as he bared his teeth in a black-whiskered grin. 'No man of honor has cause to fear Colonel Baca,' he said slowly. 'But the Senor Dios have mercy on the hombre that lies or tricks this ignorant pelado. It's better for you to relax if you are possessed of a clear conscience, Senor.'

Jefe Guzman looked sick as his fat hands spread in a gesture, the rubies like warts of fresh blood against the flesh. 'Where are you bound for?' he croaked.

'I am the Villista Colonel in command, so I go to take my place ahead of my men.'

The skull-faced Aleman Major's skeleton hand was clamped down across the Jefe's right hand that was on his Luger. 'That checks all bets,' came the toneless voice from the skull-head. 'Don't act like a damned fool, Guzman! You overbet your hand. The Villista waited until the chips were down, then he raked in the jackpot and pushed back his chair.'

The skeleton hand pulled Guzman back into the tent, and the flap dropped into place to curtain the two men. The death-head Aleman Major filled the telescope silver cup to the brim and downed the drink. The cold eyes burned into Guzman's muddy stare like dry ice.

'You told me you had these ignorant men eating out of your hand,' the Major said. His toneless voice had an ominous sound. 'Looks like that Villista bit the hand that's been feeding the pelados this—this crap.' He picked up the propaganda pamphlet and tore it to shreds, like he was ripping human flesh, dropping the residue on Guzman's high boots.

'I had them all like this.' Jefe Guzman squeezed his fleshy hands together in a twisting motion, the gleam of the red rubies mocking them both. 'The paddle-footed peons and the pelados.'

The hands came apart, and he wiped the

sweaty palms across his fat rump and reached for the bottle. 'Then something happened—overnight. That Villista showed up out of nowhere to take command.' The neck of the bottle rattled against the lip of the silver cup. 'Just when I figured I'd won something when Pablo showed up with the Mexican recruits, with the story that he'd wiped out a troop of Federalista cavalry under the command of Captain Vidal. He had proof of the massacre.' He downed his drink at a gulp. 'Something has gone wrong with the Aleman Plan,' he finished lamely.

'That stupid son of yours walked into a Texan trap, for one thing. He's still going around in a drunken haze.'

'Those damned Texans have been beating up Noel, trying to make him talk.'

'Nobody but a woman did that catclaw job on that precious, pampered son of yours, Guzman. I warned you, and I warned Noel—stay clear of women. Noel tried to make love to a she-wildcat and got the worst of it. You would do well to profit by it, Guzman.'

'Get back in your place.' Jefe Guzman's congested eyes were murderous. The thick hand fumbled at the Luger until it slid free of its holster. 'Enough of that talk. Know your place, you jailbird.'

The cold eyes of the Major glinted mockingly as they looked into the black muzzle of the Luger. The lipless mouth spread.

'Death would be welcome to a man with cancer gnawing at his guts, Guzman. Pull the trigger.' His skeleton hands were steady as he filled the silver cup, deliberately turning his back on the angered Jefe.

'If that son of yours has the guts and the brains, Guzman, he can lead that bunch into a death trap. He would, of course, die with the stupid pelados, but he lacks the guts to die an Aleman hero.'

'What kind of talk is this, you depraved jailbird?' Guzman roared.

'I was a high-ranking officer before I spent those years in prison. You would do well to remember that, General.' The Major turned around slowly, the filled cup steady in his hand. 'It would be well to remember that you, Guzman, come from a mixture of bad blood. Your father was one of a boatload of criminals who were chained together like beasts in the hold of a ship. You have surrounded yourself with men and women who are the offspring of that criminal scum, dumped somewhere on the shores of Mexico. Those are your so-called Alemans who were spawned on the sand.

'Because you were a cut above the rest in criminal brains and ruthless blood, Guzman, you murdered every man who was a threat to your growing power along the border. No polish can ever cover the blood your boots have stomped in to trample the dead you have murdered to become Jefe of the land you plan to steal from a widow.

'Kurt Guzman, king of the underworld, whose money is stained with human blood, steeped in the stench of marijuana and opium smoke, rotten with the narcotics your smugglers run across the border and sell to dope peddlers. General Kurt Guzman, Jefe of Alemanda! I salute you!' A flick of the bony wrist sent the contents of the silver cup into the fleshy face.

Guzman backed away, dropping the Luger to wipe with both hands at his eyes that were stinging, half-blinded, by the raw kummel.

The death's-head man in the gray uniform stood back and away from Guzman as his bulk slumped down on the canvas cot that threatened to collapse under the sagging weight. He leaned forward, his dripping face in his hands and the twin rubies winking in mockery of the man who had been stripped of everything that he had built up for a false empire.

The Major, whose words had flayed and scourged Guzman, stood there like a fleshless symbol of death. The icy eyes, in the skull-like face, watched with sadistic satisfaction as Guzman's heavy body shook, and terrible dry sobs ripped from the throat and slack mouth of the Jefe of Alemanda.

The tall skeleton man stood stiffly, bootheels together. The uniform became the outcast, who was nameless in a foreign land, without rank, save for this false rank in a false empire built on a rotten foundation. Strangely, the uniform added stature to the man as he stood there, looking down without pity or hate or even contempt, because the soldier standing there had purged himself of the poison that was deep inside his entrails along with the hellish rat teeth gnawing inside him. When the needle-sharp fangs ceased gnawing, it would be a sign of death and time for him to rest his skeleton fleshless bones on the ground for the last time. That was the only meaning death had for this man who had once had the prefix title of nobility. It had been a long time. Baron Von—

Jefe Guzman, his craven self-pity worn out with the last audible long sigh, straightened up with a sluggish, slothlike heaviness, his large paunch sagging between thick legs. The bloodshot eyes looked up at the man who had lashed and stripped him of all his tarnished power and ruthless and arrogant, ignorant pride in himself. A slow hate for the man who had done this to him crept into Guzman's red-veined, congested muddy eyes. His Luger pistol lay between his feet. His eyes were fixed on the skull-face while he leaned slowly forward, and his fingers closed over the wooden stock of the gun.

The skull-faced man was motionless, lifeless. Only the cold dry ice of his eyes gave any semblance of life. He waited until Jefe Guzman's heavy thumb released the safety on the Luger.

Then the Major shot Guzman between the eyes. The blinding spurt of gun flame was the final thing Kurt Guzman saw on earth.

Skull-face stood motionless, as he had stood before, the blue cordite smoke wisping into nothing from the muzzle of his pistol. His eyes held no expression as he watched the dead man pitch slowly forward, the dead weight upsetting the canvas cot, sending it backward into the wall of the tent.

Rolling dead, the heavy body lay on its back, its mountainous paunch lifted somehow obscenely. The small round hole in the forehead was filled with sluggish thick blood. The muddy eyes were glazed over with the film of death.

Skull-face slid his gun back into its holster. He filled the silver cup and drank slowly until the cup was empty. Then he turned and went outside to stand alone.

The sun was lowering toward the broken skyline. He stared into the brassy ball, unwinking, as if to take from it its last warmth before it sank. It was like he was in need of its life and final warmth to carry him toward some distant place that held no warmth. He stood, facing west, until the sun went down.

He unsaddled and turned loose the horse Jefe Guzman had ridden here. Then he mounted his own horse and rode alone at a long, high trot toward the town of Alemanda, to the army barracks there, where the soldiers he had been training were waiting without a commander.

A single star picked him up out of the moonless night to guide him to a final destiny. The man knew that death would soon release him from earthly bondage, and that the star was guiding him to that rendezvous with death. He asked nothing from death, knowing that he would meet it eagerly and unafraid. He asked only if he had a choice in the matter, that it come before dawn and dimmed the star that was guiding him.

There was still time enough left to accomplish the task that lay ahead, but no time to spare, because the night was closing in on him, and it seemed as if a black shroud was being drawn slowly across the night sky to cover the bright stars that were the eyes of the night. It seemed to the man as he rode along that whatever the night held would be too shameful in its ruthless brutality for those bright stars above to look down on.

Then came a moment of dread fear. What if the death he had held so long in his guts was creeping, crawling over him now to blind the stars that were blotting out? What if this strange phenomenon of the night was for him and him alone? There was no storm approaching. The sky had been without a cloud. It could be that the night sky was filled with stars for other men.

With the fat Guzman dead and his cowardly miserable slobbering son held captive by the verdammter esel fool of a dunce of a stinking Villista, Satan had given him the power of the black night to work the total destruction of these men who had failed in their stupidity to recognize him as a man far superior in breeding and intellect. These men would pay for their stupidity, as fat swine Guzman had paid. He had seen the horrible fear of dying in Guzman's eyes that split-second before death came, but first he had stripped the fat pig of his glory.

Not only that, Guzman had died believing that his stupid blundering had sent his precious son either to death or shameful disgrace. Guzman had figured on Noel's showing up with his arrogant swagger and bluster. Between the two, the father who called himself a general and rigged himself out in a uniform of his own designing, and his mongrel son, fitted into the same ridiculous uniform, they would assume command and put the Villista Colonel, who flaunted his ignorance and stupidity, in his place among the pelados.

Noel, however, had shown up with a woman's claw marks on his face, shame and disgrace showing in his eyes, along with fear. That in itself had been the severest blow of all to the great Guzman, whose blundering son had been his pride and joy.

The Villista had gotten rid of Noel before there had been time for Jefe Guzman to make a program of treachery, and Noel had left with the self-pitying conviction that he was being sent as human sacrifice for his father's swollen, bloated ambition.

The arsenal and ammunition dump was located a mile from the town of Alemanda. This nameless exile had himself designed its structure and had personally overseen the construction of it, down to the last detail. It was a deep, cellar-like hole in the ground, walled and floored and roofed with concrete, the roof supported by steel girders. An enclosed wireless station was atop the roof.

The inside walls of the arsenal were lined with wooden gun racks that bristled with rifles that had been cleaned and polished with Aleman efficiency. Naked bayonets gleamed in shining rows above the rifle racks. In an adjoining room, the machine guns were lined along the walls, set up on tripods and ready for instant use. The rifles and machine guns were kept fully loaded. The ammunition was stored in a separate room away from the arsenal, separated by steel doors, as were the hand grenades.

The entire concrete cellar was lighted by strings of electric bulbs overhead and controlled by a pair of master switches, one inside and one on the outside. These lights burned continuously.

A ten-foot high fence, set back a hundred yards from this concrete structure, surrounded the place. Two armed guards stood four-hour shifts on perpetual guard duty at the big gate, a sentry box on either side of the gateway.

Nobody was admitted without a written pass signed by Jefe Guzman or his son, or by the nameless Major, who used the black cross for a mark. Any man who tried to force his way in was shot down.

Mines were sprinkled along the fence at spaced intervals. In case the enemy surrounded the place and closed in for a sudden, concentrated attack, they could be blown into scattered bits. By throwing a switch, an entire army could be wiped out.

Besides the Japanese expert who attended the wireless, there was an Aleman machine gunner stationed in a pillbox outside the wireless station door. Both these men knew the location of the switch that could touch off the mines.

Only three men knew where another secret switch was located above the heavy steel door that led to the underground concrete cellar. This switch was ingeniously disguised by a foot-square replica of the Aleman flag that had been painted on the lid of a metal box, countersunk in the concrete with the deadly switch inside the box. The push button that opened the lid was in the exact center of the black cross on the scarlet Japanese sun. This switch was inside the cellar above the door and could blow the combined arsenal and ammunition dump into total destruction. Of the three men aware of its location only two remained alive. The skull-faced exile, who had designed and wired it, and Colonel Noel Guzman. The third man lay on his back in a tent with a bullet hole between his sightless eyes.

Noel Guzman, if he had the courage of a true martyr, could lead the Villistas, all who could be crowded in, inside the cellar, then open the box, throw the switch, and be blown up in heroic death.

There was an ingenious alarm system at the sentry gate. Either sentry could step on a button inside his box that would send the signal by underground cable to the wireless station where it would touch off a code signal tapped out by the sentry's boot. Both the Japanese and the Aleman machine gunner had orders, upon hearing the alarm, to throw the switch, located inside the wireless station, that would set off the mines.

Perhaps if Noel Guzman worked it cleverly, he could talk the Villista into surrounding the fence, letting the sentry give the alarm, then run for it before the mines blew up.

Noel Guzman, the verdammter coward, however, possessed no quality of such courage.

The man with the skull face knew that the verdammter swine would order the sentries on duty to open the gates for him to enter. He would hand out the guns and ammunition. The fat swine would crawl and whine and beg for his life, at any cost.

It was the skull-faced man's destiny to accomplish that which Noel Guzman lacked the courage to do. The trick of it was to get there before the Villistas, guided by the craven Noel Guzman, arrived.

The Villistas were traveling on foot. The mounted Colonel Baca and Noel Guzman would perforce be slowed down.

Satan himself had given him the major blackness of this night to cloak his movements. It was a mile's march from the barracks at the edge of town to the arsenal. He would order them to stack rifles at the barracks, and rearm when they reached the arsenal with new rifles from the arsenal. He would remove the gate sentries, instruct his sergeants to lock the gates when the Villistas were inside the fence, and he would be waiting there in the wireless station.

He, himself, with his two skeleton hands, would pull the switch to explode the mines and then step outside to watch the blast of flame that would shoot into the sky, sending hundreds of Villistas to their death. Contemplating what he would do gave this man complete satisfaction.

The blast of destruction should be timed for around midnight, at the latest. That should give him ample time to carry his program of hate to final completion before dawn paled his star.

He was thinking, as he spurred his horse to the limit, how the Aleman Plan belonged to him, a nameless man without a country; the germ of the plan born of a warped sadistic brain. He recalled how he had suggested to Kurt Guzman a program to perpetuate the Aleman race. The plan had pleased the exile who had been dumped on a foreign land to die, with holes eaten in his guts and his lungs gone.

Guzman had immediately named what the major had mapped out the Guzman Aleman Plan. Verdammter Dumkopf!

Then came the flag and the uniforms and the ranks. 'What rank did you hold?' the fat swine had asked when he was handing out military rank.

'Does it matter?' he had answered.

'You shall be a Major,' the Jefe decided.

Now Skull-face was commander-in-chief, an overnight monarch who would be blown to hell this dark night, if he lived long enough to carry to fulfillment his program of hate.

Even the Villista Colonel, who took an earthy pride in his status as a penniless, ignorant Indian, had seen through the Aleman Plan. This pelado had taunted the Jefe and his son, mocked them and made fools of them, not knowing that he, too, before the night was ended, would be destroyed and his pelados along with him.

The night hid the madman's hideous grin as he looked skyward. The grin was still there on his skull-face as the ice came into his guts. Verdammter Gott! The star was no longer in the solid, heavy, black sky that was lowering like a shroud to smother him. The thin, whistling sound that came from behind clenched teeth was lost in the blackness. It was as if he was back in the dungeon, his eyes blinded forever. Panic gripped him. Nein! To go blind on this final night, when he had need of that star, above all else.

He fumbled in the pocket of his tunic until he found matches. The match flame seared his eyes. The harsh laughter had the sound of a death-rattle as he held the flame cupped in front of his eyes till the matchstick burned out. The image of the flame was retained and he rode with it, raking the horse with his spurs. He unscrewed the cork on a silver flask and drank without tasting the raw kummel, until he felt it burn into his guts to thaw the ice. A second and third match flame to light the way to the fulfillment of his program of hate, spurring blindly ahead. Then the big black horse stumbled and went down, somersaulting in the darkness, throwing its rider clear. The animal had been ridden to death.

The dark closed in his plight. He drained the last drop of kummel and threw the flask away. He struck his last match and held it before his eyes as he stumbled on through the black night, his quickening gasp making a hissing sound through bared teeth as his skeleton hands clawed the dark wall of the arsenal a mile from Alemanda.

His arms lifted, and an animal cry was torn from his skull-like face. 'The Star! The Star!' Blood spewed, and the cough raked the skeleton frame as he staggered on.

When he reached the gate, pulling himself together, he instructed the two sentries to leave their posts, and when they had gone he made his way to the wireless station, where he gave the Japanese and the Aleman gunner the same orders to leave. He knew now that he would not live long enough to await the arrival of the Villistas and Noel Guzman. His program of hate would go unfinished.

Time was running short for the nameless exile. He must hurry if he expected to explode the mines and arsenal. Using the last of his ebbing strength, blood spewing into his mouth from internal hemorrhage, he would pull the switch that would explode the mines, paying no attention to the curtain of flame that filled the black night. He made his way to the concrete cellar and pushed the button on the Aleman flag to open the secret switch box. He pulled the handle to explode the arsenal and ammunition, letting out a harsh, grating sound when the heavy explosion and the curtain of fire engulfed him.

CHAPTER NINE

As they left the Villista camp, Bass and young Pablo riding alongside each other, Bass slid the six-shooter from under his shirt, holding it down between his lean belly and his saddle horn, with the gun pointed at Pablo's belly.

'Just so you won't get any fool notions, hombre,' Bass grinned flatly. 'About takin' me to any Aleman jailhouse.'

'You can put the gun away, Tejano,' Pablo's eyes matched the sullen tone of his voice. 'Your men are waiting in a barracana a mile from here. I am taking you to join them.'

Pablo twisted his head to meet Bass' cold gray eyes. 'That paper you would have me read back in the tent,' the young Mexican said, his voice brittle. 'That first paragraph was the Aleman Oath. Therefore, I refused to read the words aloud.'

'Jefe Guzman didn't swear you in, then?' asked Bass.

'He had the mistaken notion that his swine of a son had already sworn me in when I rode with those peon Alemans into the barracks at Alemanda.' Pablo smiled thinly and commenced rolling a cigarette. 'It was Dona Catalina who sent me back across the river with the peon Aleman recruits. Yaqui and a few of the Santa Catalina vaqueros came along.

'One of your Tejanos sent a wireless message to the Ranger station at Palofox saying that you had been captured by the Villistas. Dona Catalina was in Palofox when the message came in. Yaqui volunteered to go back into Mexico when she told him about it. He called the names of those he wanted to take along. My name was not spoken.' Pablo lit his cigarette. 'I sat squatted on my bootheels with a bottle. I was hoping that the Alemans or Villistas would kill you.'

Pablo's white teeth showed through the tobacco smoke. 'Then I felt the point of a very sharp knife between my shoulder blades. When I turned my head, there was that damned girl in the yellow dress, that Pepa. Madre de Dios? That she-wildcat!

'"You killed my brother El Capitan Vidai," she said. "The knife I hold is going into your gizzard, my Pablocita, unless you spring to your feet and volunteer to go with Yaqui and take your peon Aleman soldiers with you. Arise, Pablocito, or this knife will be twisted inside your entrails."' Pablo's laugh was short and bitter.

'So I am here as you perceive, but, por Dios, I had no choice in the matter.'

Bass chuckled and slid his gun into its scabbard.

'My only desire was to get away from that Pepa Vidal,' Pablo added. 'But no! That one came along.' Pablo said with disgust. 'She emerged wearing an Aleman uniform, and it was Pepa that the Colonel dispatched to fetch Noel Guzman. You yourself saw the condition in which the Colonel arrived.

'Pepa is with your Tejanos now, strutting around in that Aleman uniform, making eyes at the one who has the wireless, calling him Frijole Beanses in a love-sick voice. Pepa makes a joke out of everything, and the Tejanos laugh, but I do not laugh, Senor. I do not care to be alone with that one.

'Madre de Dios! One night long ago when Pepa was dancing and singing her love songs, I got very borracho, so drunk that I make love to that Pepa. She swears I ask her to marry me, and she is holding me to that promise.'

Pablo eyed the bottle of golden tequila in the pocket of Bass' chaps. 'Behold you a man with cold misery in the guts. That Pepa Vidal has dwelt upon the subject, describing our marriage with that knife she packs between us, the cold steel of the blade to chill the love that should be warm. That knife is needle-pointed, and the blade is honed to the sharpness of a razor.'

Pablo spread his hands in a gesture of utter despair. 'You look upon a young man in the prime of life with the shadow of death upon him. It is indeed a thing of pity for me to die so young.'

'I'll be sure to spill a tear,' Bass said carelessly. 'No doubt Pepa will pay for a Mass.'

'You make a joke of misfortune, Senor.'

'What else?' Bass gouged bits of cork from the neck of the bottle with a knife blade. 'What would you have me do, man?'

'Get that Pepa to release me from a promise of which I have no recollection, Senor. Por favor.'

'So you can get drunk and lie for me in ambush with that silver-mounted gun, thinking if this Tejano was dead Dona Catalina's daughter would perhaps marry you? I'm no fool, hombre. A man and a caballero worthy of the name keeps his given word. Drunkenness is never used as an excuse.'

Bass poked the remains of the cork inside the bottle, holding it against the last rays of sunset to admire the golden color that meant the stuff was well aged. Out of the tail of his eye, he saw Pablo run his tongue across his dry lips.

'Where I come from,' Bass said, 'a man drinks only with friends, from the same bottle. This is damn good tequila. Whiskers on it.'

'Madre de Dios, Senor!' Pablo pleaded. 'Am I not down here to fight alongside you against the Alemans?'

'You'd be drinking in a cantina on the other

side of the Rio Grande, hombre, but for Pepa.'

'Now that I am here, I will fight with you, Senor, not against you. Be assured of that!'

'Strictly from necessity. I hope you won't be underfoot.' Bass shoved the bottle at Pablo. 'Don't start calling me companero, till you have proved you got a right to.' Bass rolled a cigarette. 'You and Pepita should make a handsome couple, Pablo.'

Pablo choked and coughed. 'You do not perhaps understand the senoritas of Mexico? Rest assured, Pepa means what she says. She will hold me to my foolish promise, and she will choose to wait until she is ready before she slides the knife blade into my insides.' He took a couple of swallows.

'I'm willing to take the word of a caballero who's been around. You shore know your women, Pablo.'

'Too well,' Pablo conceded. 'But not too wisely.' The light of hope was in his eyes. 'If you would get Pepita to release me from that promise, Senor, I would gladly relinquish all claim to the daughter of Dona Catalina. That I swear by the silver gun that is a heritage of honor.'

'I'll hold the thought, Pablo,' Bass told him as they rode into the brushy barranco, already deep in the shadow of the coming night.

The Texans were squatted in a wide circle around a small fire. Pepa, in the baggy, outsized Aleman uniform, the trouser legs and sleeves rolled high, was slapping out tortillas. Dutch ovens and blackened coffee pots simmered on a bed of coals. Pepita was singing a ranchero song.

Beans was hunkered alongside the wireless set, the earphones across his shock of uncombed, sandy hair. Pecos got to his feet, the slow grin on his leathery face was the only welcome Bass needed as he swung to the ground.

Pepa dropped the thin tortilla, the plaintive song ending in a squeal. She ran, flinging her arms around Bass' neck, plastering his face with moist kisses.

'It shore beats hell,' drawled a Texan voice. 'The luck some fellers have.'

'That is por the Senorita Kit Crawford.' Pepa tossed back her black mane. 'Por myself, I wait till the moonlight.' She rolled her eyes toward Beans. Then she saw Pablo, who was behind his horse, unsaddling.

'Oh, hah!' She cried out. 'You are in hiding, no?' She whirled and picked up the knife that lay on the ground where she had been sitting.

There was no handshaking, no demonstration of welcome. Bass unsaddled and turned his horse loose and walked over to where Beans squatted. 'Any news from the Ranger Station at Palofox, Beans?' His words fell heavily on the hushed silence.

Pecos had come up alongside Bass and gripped his shoulder. 'We've got a little bad news, Bass,' Pecos said quietly. 'Seems like Kate Crawford and her daughter Kit have been kidnapped by Lobo Jones and his curly wolves.'

Bass headed, without a word, for the nearest saddled horse that stood with reins dropped, ground tied. Just then the giant Yaqui rode up.

The big man had shed the Aleman uniform and was dressed in vaquero clothes. 'When I returned to kill Jefe Guzman with the Luger pistol,' he told Bass, 'he was already dead. I guess that Aleman with the dead skull for a face had shot him between the eyes and left him.'

'You better break the news to him, Bass,' Pecos said. 'Yaqui don't know.'

The giant Yaqui took it wooden-faced. Only the eyes showed what went on inside him, the bitterness and the hatred were there.

Pecos already had Bass' saddle on a fresh horse. Beans was busy scrawling a message on his pad.

'That was the Ranger Station at Palofox, Bass,' Beans said. 'Captain Clay McCoy turned in his commission as Captain of the Texas Rangers today. He was just sighted crossing the river on his blue mule.'

Bass nodded and mounted his horse. Pepa shoved a large tortilla, wrapped around beans, into Bass' hand. 'That is what's called a burro. Eat it as you ride,' she said.

Bass ate the bean burro mechanically, without tasting it, as he rode away, with Pecos on one side and Pepa on his other flank. They followed Yaqui, who rode in the lead.

The Mexican girl had dropped a little behind, to let Bass and Pecos ride together, and Bass was grateful for her thoughtfulness.

Right now Bass Slocum McCoy was not proud of himself. In his own bleak eyes he made a sorry picture as he tried to calculate and weigh himself to find out the kind of a man he had turned out to be.

What he was thinking must have shown for Pecos to see, because he spoke in that quiet way he had. 'You are packin' a hell of a lot of things in that load you've been totin' around, Bass, that don't belong there. There's no use hoggin' all the blame, boy.

'I rode the outlaw trail with your daddy, Tom Slocum, and Bill Crawford before you were born. Ranger Captain Clay McCoy had to kill your daddy or get killed. He beat Slocum to his gun. He gave wild Bill Crawford his chance to go straight, and if ever a man had a chance to steady down it was Bill Crawford. But in the end, when he failed to keep his word, Clay McCoy gave him an even break and shot him.

'I came into Mexico after that, and several months ago the Ranger Captain sent me word that he'd scratch out the old indictment against me if I'd fetch you to Palofox to stand trial. He'd found out after you left that the stranger you shot in self-defense had killed a young Ranger and was wearing his shirt, an' left the Ranger identification on the neckband.

'McCoy wanted me to bring you across the Rio Grande to stand trial and clear your name of a murder charge, but I kept putting it off, because I figured you wasn't ready to go back and shake hands with that psalm-shoutin' Ranger Captain.

'Mebbyso I should've laid it on the line for you six months ago. Mebbyso we wouldn't be in this tight fix tonight,' Pecos ended up.

'I'd have balked at the notion six months ago,' Bass said flatly. 'But I'm seeing a lot of things tonight that I have never taken a look at up till now. It's all mixed up, an' I got to work it out for myself. It's like ridin' through a big herd and cuttin' back the strays that don't belong. Right now, seems like I'm a green hand, an' I don't know the brands.'

'You'll make out,' the grizzled Pecos told him. 'The same as that Yaqui up ahead. He's takin' the blame for ever leavin' those two women. Spite of the fact that Kate sent him to dicker with the Yaquis for your hide. Cattle Kate swapped 'em most of the land to set you free. Until he's got 'er made, one way or the other, you stay away from him, boy, because right now he's also blamin' you, because he was sent to bring you back.'

'I know,' Bass nodded. 'That adds up. Just

one more rotten mark to go down in the tally book.'

'Another thing, boy,' Pecos said. 'Forget about these Texans. Quit takin' the blame. If they had a choice, they wouldn't be no other place than where they are.' Pecos tilted his head to look up at the sky and the dimming stars. 'There's one hell of a dust storm somewheres. I sighted it along the skyline at sundown. An hour from now, there won't be a star in the sky, an' you won't be able to see your hand in front of you. When it gets that dark we'll stay close-bunched. It's a good night to get plumb lost.'

Pecos said something about telling the rest of the Texans to stay close-bunched, and with a final warning to Bass not to lose himself, the grizzled Texan dropped back to let Bass ride his troubles out alone.

Bass found some solace in the black night that shut him off from the world. It eased some of the tight coils of the spring that had been screwed and wound too tight inside him. Pecos had told him facts tonight that gave him a broader understanding of things. He had explained, from the viewpoint of an outlaw, the way of a Texas Ranger.

Pecos held no animosity against Captain Clay McCoy, who had run him out of Texas. Pecos had done a lot to clear up the air regarding the killing of his outlaw father, and Bill Crawford.

It was not so much in the things Pecos had said, as it was in what he had left out, that gave Bass to understand that the grizzled outlaw had a high regard for Clay McCoy, both as a man and as a Texas Ranger. Pecos had not praised or eulogized the Ranger Captain because he had a notion or intention of influencing the younger man in any way. Pecos was leaving that strictly up to Bass and his own beliefs. According to the lights of the grizzled Pecos, a man was not worth the salt of his keep or the gunpowder to blow him to hell, unless that man had a code of his own to live up to.

That close-mouthed, iron-gray outlaw had spoken tonight for the first time. Until now Bass had not been aware that he had ridden with Tom Slocum, or that Tom Slocum and Bill Crawford had ridden the outlaw trail together, and Pecos along with them. Tonight he learned for the first time that Ranger Clay McCoy had killed Wild Bill Crawford, and he wondered if Bill's widow was aware of that fact. It was the general belief that Bill Crawford had been killed by Mexicans from the Santa Catalina Grant, to gain the reward offered by Don Luis de la Guerra.

Remembering back now, from little things Dona Catalina had hinted at, rather than spoke of outright, Bass had a hunch that the widow knew it had been Ranger Clay McCoy who killed her outlaw husband. In fact, Bass felt sure that it was the Ranger Captain himself who had broken the news to Kate Crawford, because that was a part of the strict code of his own making that he lived by.

The killing of Bill Crawford must have taken place on the Mexican side of the Rio Grande, where no Texas Ranger is allowed to cross in line of duty, because there was no written record of Bill Crawford's being shot by a Texas Ranger. Crawford's grave was at his ranch in Texas. Somebody, and Bass reckoned it was Ranger McCoy, had fetched the dead body out of Mexico to the Texas ranch.

Kate Crawford had known the facts, but she had not told Bass, and Bass reckoned Kit was ignorant of the true facts regarding the killing of her father.

If Pecos held no grudge against Captain Clay McCoy, and if Kate Crawford regarded him as a staunch, loyal friend and a man of honor, that was proof enough of the sterling worth of his foster-father as a man and a preacher of God's word and a Texas Ranger who let nothing stand between him and his line of duty.

Without effort, Bass let his memory drift back to countless things, trivial now, that had seemed vastly important at the time to his kid's way of thinking. In each one of these seemingly trivial things, Ranger Captain Clay McCoy, whom he thought of as his own father, had been justified in his stern reprimand of young Bass.

Tonight, thinking back, Bass realized how he had hurt this man who had taken him home and given him a name he could be proud of. Bass had been no worse than the rest of the kids in the tough border cowtown of Laredo, but he had gone out of his way to out-do the others because the Ranger Captain was his father.

The killing of the drunken stranger had brought it all to a climax. When Bass had learned that his real father had been an outlaw, that seemed to account for his bad behavior to both Bass and the Ranger Captain. Both had laid the blame on the heredity of bad outlaw, renegade blood. Clay McCoy had forgotten that Tom Slocum had come from a respectable family of real Texan blood lines. Tom Slocum was an outlaw because of a freak of fate. He was a wild cowboy who had gone wrong and had taken the outlaw trail.

It was only after Bass had ridden across the river into Mexico that Clay McCoy had taken the burden of guilt from Bass and carried it inside him. It had been Kate Crawford who had said to him, 'Perhaps you have been too strict, Clay. You expected, perhaps, too much from Bass. You are the finest man I have ever known, Clay, and young Bass is like you in all that stands for decency and true courage. Without his knowing it, young Bass has patterned his ways after yours. When I find him, and I'll find him somehow or other, I'll bring him back home.'

Bass knew nothing of that conversation as he rode into the night, but this much he surmised now from the things that Kate Crawford had let drop with what now, tonight, seemed like a studied, calculated carelessness, that Clay McCoy had been in love with the woman who was the widow of the outlaw he had killed. It was a love he had never put into word or gesture, and the woman had returned that love in the same unspoken manner.

Bass knew for certain now that it was Clay McCoy's love for Kate Crawford, together with a father's love for his son, that had fetched the Ranger Captain on his blue mule across the Rio Grande. That had meant, perforce, the turning in of his commission in the Texas Rangers, because as a peace officer he had no status south of the border.

With the United States at war, and Mexico in the throes of another revolution, all it would take right now would be for a Captain of the Texas Rangers to cross the Rio Grande to rescue the kidnapped women, and the echoes of the Ranger's gun would be heard at Washington. By that time it would be too late.

The Rio Grande that marked the International Border, lay like a twisted fuse between the two countries. It would take no more than a spark to touch off a powder keg, and there would be war. With the rebel army of Pancho Villa sweeping the border, and the federal government in power on its way out, the Villista raids across the border stirring up dormant enmities, it was a delicate situation.

No man knew and understood the danger better than Clay McCoy. It was his job to hold the Texans back, to pour water and sand on the conflagration flaring up along the strip of the Big Bend that was his territory. The hot-blooded Texans along the border were too eager in their readiness to prove their boast that they could take Mexico overnight, and this new Aleman threat was something the Texans wanted to tromp out, like a cowhand tromps the head of a rattlesnake into the ground with the high heel of his boot.

Bass knew that it had taken a hell of a lot to bring Clay McCoy across the river, and Bass wanted to be there to side his foster-father when the time came.

Right now, that was all that mattered. Then the thought came that Clay McCoy had been more than a father to him. More than anything on earth Bass wanted to find him and tell him so, tell him he was sorry for all the worry and grief and embarrassment and headaches he had caused him. He wanted to say that it had taken him all this time to realize and understand Clay McCoy as a man and father, as a Texas Ranger and a man who preached the word of God.

With the deep desire and sincere hope that some day he would grow into the breed of man

Clay McCoy was, came a strange feeling of security within himself. Bass knew that tonight he had reached his full manhood. Until now he had been a pistol kid, playing at being a man. He would like to hand Clay McCoy the shot-loaded end of the quirt looped around his saddle horn.

'Lay it on hard, Cap'n,' he'd say. 'Like you shoulda done a long time ago. I can savvy the lesson now.'

Bass reined up to wait for Pecos. He wanted to tell Pecos he had ridden the thing out, like he would ride a spoiled bronc. He reached for his Bull Durham and papers and rolled himself a cigarette while he waited for Pecos and the others to come up.

It was not until he had gotten the cigarette lit and partly smoked that Bass knew he was all alone in the middle of the black night. Not only that, the horse he was forking was another of the Santa Catalina palominos, foaled like as not back at the Hacienda, and he had let the horse travel on a free rein. A horse is apt to head back for home, and how long he had been traveling like that Bass had no way of knowing. All he knew was that he was lost right now, in the middle of nowhere, like some greenhorn tenderfoot, without sense of direction in the darkness.

The air was motionless, without so much as a faint breeze to guide him, to face into or turn his back to for a compass point. He could feel the dust from the far distant storm as it came into his nostrils. His teeth felt gritty with the powdery stuff that sifted down from the heavy black sky. Panic gripped him. There was a desperate need for him to be at the border town of Alemanda. His life and the lives of Clay McCoy, Kate Crawford and the redheaded Kit, the girl he loved, depended on his being there now as fast as a horse could carry him. On this night, of all nights, he had to get himself lost like a dude pilgrim, just when he had found himself.

He spat the half-smoked cigarette from his dust-filmed lips, remembering Pecos' parting warning. 'Don't get yourself lost.'

Bass slid his gun from its holster and tilting it skyward, he thumbed back the hammer, thinking how silly he would feel when the answering shots to his lost signal came back, the joshing and hoorahing he would get. He spaced three shots, counting ten seconds off between each shot.

He reloaded his gun as he waited for the answer to his signal of distress, but only the hollow, mocking echo of the three shots came back out of the opaque wall of blackness.

'You thick-skulled sorry specimen!' Bass gritted. Then the faint thread of a glimmer of hope came. What if this was one of the palominos foaled on Kate Crawford's Texas ranch? The horse was restless, rearing to go, like as not getting nervous from the tension of its rider.

'I got nothing left to lose, feller.' Bass gritted as he gave the horse a slack rein. 'Have at it.'

Bass wanted to pray, but he felt too ashamed to say the words of any prayer. He was thinking, as the horse hit a long high trot, *I'd be a mighty poor specimen if I called on God to side me in a tight spot now; this horse is packing me somewhere. I don't know where he's headed for, but I hope it's where I want to go. If I make it tonight, you got yourself another hand, regardless . . . Amen.*

Bass had said the Amen aloud. It had a strange sound in his ears. His faint grin was lost in the night as he realized he had been talking to God, as if he knew Him.

Somehow, Bass had become aware of sounds around him. There was a movement of sound, blurred and blotted in the heavy black of the night that enveloped horse and rider. The distorted sounds had a ghoulish whisper, like dead men calling out in dead voices.

A man had to depend on his ears and smell and sense of touch now, but the hissing whisper that spread all around him had the same unknown, intangible quality of the rubber-black of the night.

The palm of his hand felt sweaty on the butt of his six-shooter, and memory came of how he had ridden into the coyote trap. Now he knew what the eerie sounds were. It was the Villistas who had fanned out and were coming on moccasined feet up the valley.

From somewhere ahead, a bunch of cattle, spooked by the sounds, broke brush. Other bushed-up cattle, sensing the unknown terror of sound, stampeded. A steer bawled in fright, and other steers took it up. Range cattle are accustomed to the familiar sight of a man on horseback. A man on foot is a strange phenomenon, evil and dangerous as a wolf or tiger or mountain lion or a coyote.

There were five hundred or more Villistas dogtrotting, their numbers spread out the entire width of the valley, and Bass knew now that the line of soldiers was driving the terrified cattle up the valley in the direction of the Rio Grande. The cattle would settle down to a walk after the initial terror had played itself out.

Somewhere in the black beyond, a gun exploded. Then a few more shots. A hoarse shout lifted through the din of clashing horns and the heavy dull thudding of cloven hoofs. 'Ride the hell clear, you curly wolves! Get the bell gone! I don't know what's comin', an' I ain't lingerin' to find out. I'm headin' for town where the bossman, Lobo Jones, is drinkin' and girlin'. To hell with this!'

Bass knew where he was now. He was in the valley and headed in the right direction. So were El Lobo's curly wolves, and the Villistas on foot were driving the six thousand Santa

Catalina cattle ahead of them. They would cross the Rio Grande, and there would not be enough horse-backers to turn the big herd back. Bass told himself that this was the doing of the giant Yaqui from the Santa Catalina Rancho.

Bass calculated that he himself was behind the drag end of the running cattle, but ahead of the dog-trotting Villistas. He was headed in the general direction of Alemanda, and that was all that mattered until he got there.

* * *

Somewhere ahead, the Villista Colonel and his dozen armed soldiers spurred their horses. The Villista's grin was blacked out in the night as he spoke to Noel Guzman.

'The Senorita Pepa,' the Villista spoke into the night, 'has passed on to me the secret information you confided in her when you were borracho and inclined to boast of your superior knowledge that gives the gringo Aleman the power over the so-called stupid Indians. I am aware of the mines that are laid around the high wire fence surrounding the arsenal and ammunition dump. I know of the signal to the wireless station, to be given by the gate sentries. I am using that information and the knowledge of the mines to suit my stupid pelado strategy regarding things of a military nature.

'I am willing to let you go, Senor, after you have made safe the way for my men to get the guns and the bullets from the arsenal. I will allow you time to consider the proper methods, Senor, while I get this most stubborn cork from the long constriction of the neck of this beautiful bottle of golden tequila. Keep one thing in mind, Senor, before you put your thoughts into the scheme: I want not a single one of my men to get so much as a scratched hide when the mines blow up. Otherwise, the manner of your death will be prolonged and unpleasant.'

'I can manage it so that no harm will come to you and your men,' Noel Guzman said. 'But if I do this, what assurance have I that you will keep your end of the agreement to set me free?'

'You have my word as a man and a soldier, Senor.'

'That is not enough. I don't trust you even in daylight, and this is a dark night. You left my father behind with that crazy jailbird who was exiled from Germany. That man engineered the planting of the mines. He's crazy. I told my father to kill him or let me kill him. Now my father is left alone with that crazy convict, and that gringo Tejano is free. That verdammter son of a bitch—and that Mexican chippy who clawed my face. It would give me pleasure to have a gun in my hand if we ever meet again.' Guzman's voice shrilled in the darkness.

'Once my men have the guns and the bullets and the pesos, Senor,' said the Villista grimly, 'it will give me the extreme pleasure to send you to your barracks at Alemanda, so that you can prepare your Aleman soldiers for our attack. I, Colonel Baca of the army of Pancho Villa, will ride in the lead of the Villistas. That battle will decide once and for all the supremacy of the Aleman Uber Alles gringo soldiers against this ignorant Villista and his stupid pelados.'

They rode along in silence while the Villista struggled to get the broken cork from the bottle neck.

'I perceive the lights of the sentry boxes,' the Villista said, breaking heavy silence. 'We pull up here. I calculate the distance to be a hundred yards, just beyond range of the mines. The time has come, Senor, for you to produce. Blow up the mines, or else, no?'

'I will need a gun to give the signal to the sentries on duty.'

'I give you your own Luger, a present from the Senorita Pepa. Be extremely careful to point the gun into the sky.'

Colonel Noel Guzman thumbed the safety and tilted the barrel of the gun skyward. He pulled the trigger, counting aloud, 'Ein, schwei, drei, fier.' When he had counted up to ten, he fired six shots. He said, 'That's the signal warning the sentries of the enemy approach. If the sentries obey orders, they will send the alarm to the wireless station. The mines will be exploded from there.'

When a few minutes dragged, and there was no explosion, Noel Guzman broke out in a cold sweat. He and the Villista sighted the two sentries as they left the lighted sentry boxes on a run. The Villista had the bottle tilted, when the blinding glare of the exploding mines curtained the blackness. They were within radius of its glare.

'Adios, Colonel Noel Guzman.' The Villista raised his voice above the last echoes of the blast 'Have your Aleman soldiers in readiness. Tonight Colonel Baca and his pelados are taking the town of Alemanda! Adios! Get the hell out of my eyes!'

As Guzman spurred his horse into the night, he looked back across his shoulder to watch the second explosion that would blow the arsenal and ammunition dump into the sky. When that came, it should bury the stupid Villista and his dozen mounted soldiers with the debris; kill and cripple both men and horses.

Before the Aleman Colonel was out of hearing range, the whole world seemed to explode. Men and horses were knocked down. The blinding flame of the blast was everywhere. The Villista shouted orders to run as he spurred his own horse to escape the falling debris of shattered concrete that fell from the sky.

When the blast spent itself, the Villista Colonel filled the air with blasphemy. Only a huge black crater, filled with burning, twisted debris, remained of the promised guns and bullets.

Colonel Baca promised his men, 'We will take the cursed town of Alemanda. I, myself, will attend to that Aleman lying dog.'

CHAPTER TEN

Bass reined up with a jerk as the sheet of flame splashed against the black wall of the night, more vivid than lightning, the heavy thudding roar of the explosions following a few seconds later than the flashes. Bass knew that the arsenal and ammunition dump and the mines around the wire fence had been blown up.

In the slim half-light of the explosion, yellowish in the dust haze, Bass could see the entire valley ahead filled with moving cattle, shuffling to the Rio Grande that lay a mile or so beyond. Behind the restless sea of longhorned cattle came the thin line of men, dog-trotting at a steady, tireless gait, the nearest no more than a hundred yards away. They were hatless with a white band tied around their foreheads, stripped to the waist, the naked blades of the heavy machetes slung from belts. A lot of them held dried gourds in their hands, and it was these gourds, with the seeds rattling inside, that had made the hissing sound of rattlesnakes in the dark.

Bass twisted in his saddle to find Yaqui from the Santa Catalina Grant, riding back from the moving herd and the line of runners. Yaqui held the Luger pistol in his hand.

Bass' gelding nickered, and Yaqui's answered. As Yaqui reined up, the horses nuzzled each other. The glare of the blast had faded out as suddenly as it had appeared, and the last rumbling echo of the explosion came through the darkness that seemed blacker than before.

'The lead steers of the herd,' Yaqui said, flat-toned, 'are already at the river bank. Nothing can stop them now. By daylight the entire herd should be across the river.'

Yaqui cupped a match flame in one hand to light the cigarette in a corner of his lipless mouth, and Bass saw the glitter of the black eyes in a dark face. The match stick burned itself out in Yaqui's hand before he spoke again.

'That is how the Yaqui runners with rattles accomplish in one night what your Tejanos would require a week to complete. They spooked the cattle from the brush and into the open to take the trail to water.'

Bass sensed something in the toneless voice that tightened his grip on his six-shooter. The words, spat like a bad taste into the blackness, held bitterness, hatred, contempt and loathing for all mankind that was not pure Yaqui. The giant Yaqui, who had been held all these years in serfdom, was peeling and shucking off with every word, the crusted sweat of days and months and years, here in the black night. He was cutting and splintering and whittling off all the baseness of humiliation born of long servitude, to get to the core of a once-splendid fierce pride.

Generations ago the pure Indian blood of this giant Yaqui had been that of a proud, unconquered people, with their own religion and written records of kings who were called Chiefs, and the fierce, proud blood of this man who spoke in the darkness was of that pure bloodline that was no more. Perhaps the speaker of dark words was the last of a once-splendid dynasty.

Bass knew this, somehow, as he remembered the man's heroic stature, the proud cut to the dark features and the blackness of his eyes.

'The young Mexican Pablo,' Yaqui continued, 'is again the Major Domo in charge of the Santa Catalina vaqueros. He is with them now and will remain in full charge.

'When the Yaqui runners have shoved the last of the cattle to where the Major Domo can handle them, the Yaquis will disappear as they came in the night, because their debt to Dona

Catalina will be paid in full.

'The Villista Colonel in charge of the Yaquis, was born of a Yaqui mother and Mexican father, who was a general. When Colonel Baca has accomplished his purpose of supplying guns and cartridges to the Yaquis, he will be of no further use. He will rejoin Pancho Villa and his army to follow his career as a soldier.

'When I leave here, I will go to where he is, to take the leadership of the Yaquis from the Villista and take my peoole home, because I am now Chief of the Yaquis. I came from a bloodline of Chiefs before me. While my father still lived, the brand of a Mexican was burned into my chest. When I would have destroyed myself in order not to bear the brand of shame and disgrace, the daughter of a Mexican called de la Guerra stood in front of me to take the bullets of her father's firing squad. I had no desire to live in bondage, but the little girl gave me no choice. My life belonged to that girl.

'Then you came. Senor Bass, with your Tejanos, and Dona Catalina took her daughter and the Santa Catalina Mexicans with her across the Rio Grande into Texas. Dona Catalina freed me there. She gave me a legal document that transferred title to the Santa Catalina Grant to the Yaqui Indians.

'She did not make it a command that I find you and set you free. It was a request and a prayer, and I gave her my promise, remembering that I was banished from my people, because I wore a Mexican brand of disgrace.

'I am telling you these things so that you will understand, because I am handing into your care and responsibility Dona Catalina and her daughter. Where my bondage was put on with a branding iron, in hatred and contempt, yours is a bondage of love. But don't misunderstand me, Senor Bass, I hold only a deep regard for Dona Catalina and her daughter.'

'That is understood.' Bass dared speak for the first time.

'The Tejano has this thing called a wireless, to send messages. The Yaquis possess no such magic which talks through miles of air across mountains and desert and wide rivers, but we have means of communication, and the word has come to me that Dona Catalina and her daughter are held prisoners on an island by the smugglers of contraband. This El Lobo has made use of it. It is an island covered with heavy brush. Perhaps you are aware of such an island, Senor? It is called Isla Diablo.'

'I know of the island.' Bass spoke dimly into the darkness.

'It was this gringo called El Lobo who kidnapped both women. That is all I know concerning it. The information came from one of the men my Yaqui runners captured an hour ago.'

'I'd like to talk to this man,' Bass said.

'The man is now dead, Senor,' Yaqui replied. 'It is now time for me to go to my people, and for you to join your Tejanos I hear coming through the brush. I have never taken any man's hand in friendship, until now.' Yaqui's hand closed over Bass' hand as it lay on the saddle horn.

Bass felt the grip of the big hand that could have crushed his bones. The pressure was firm and strong, as the man was strong in his new pride.

'I have met Captain Clay McCoy,' Yaqui said. 'He is a father to be proud of, and you are a son worthy of such a father. Therefore, I leave Dona Catalina and her daughter in your hands. Adios, Senor Bass.'

'Adios, Yaqui.'

As Yaqui rode away into the night, Bass' Texans rode out of the brush. Pepita was with them. She was singing one of her ranchero songs, a love song of the Mexican people. She was singing to the lanky Beans and to no other man on earth.

Bass and his Texans rode toward the town of Alemanda.

The terrific impact of the blown-up arsenal and ammunition dump had shaken the town of Alemanda. Places that boasted plate glass windows now had the shattered glass to sweep out, or let lie. Some of the adobe buildings had been severely shaken. Walls had crumbled, and roofs caved in. The walls of the power plant on the river had buckled by the tremor, and the electric power had been cut off, leaving the town in total darkness.

The dust pall that had hung over the town was saturated by the pungent stench of burnt cordite and gunpowder that had sifted down from the explosion.

The dark night was filled with the excited cursing and shouting of the drunken Aleman soldiers. The enemy was at hand, hence the extreme, desperate, last means of the blown-up arsenal. The Aleman soldiers, bewildered and confused by lack of a leader, mixed and shouted as they shoved and tromped their way in the black night, toward the armory where their guns were stacked. When they reached the armory they found only the adobe walls standing, the roof caved in to bury their rifles.

Half a dozen fires broke out in the buildings that lined the wide street. The angry red glow of the fires spread across the town, lying there like a sub-strata under the heavy smoke pall that weighted it down, holding it there and spreading it like a film of blood.

Men and women moved aimlessly in their confusion and one looked like another from a distance, like so many animals moving without direction. Fear of what lay beyond in the black night held them trapped there in the red glow.

'Looks like a place to stay away from,' Bass called to Pecos as they rode in the lead of the

Texans. He reined up and waited for the rest to catch up, loosening the saddlebags.

'You take those saddlebags, Beans,' he told the lanky, sandy-haired Beans. 'Take Pepita with you when you cross the river. Take the saddlebags to the Ranger headquarters. You and Pepita stay there. Get gone while the going's good.'

Bass and Pecos and the others rode cautiously into town, keeping well in the black shadows, silent, grim-faced, hard-eyed Texans with their guns in their hands.

Bass let out a gritty sound. He pointed with the barrel of his guns toward a big blue mule and the man on its back. It was Captain Clay McCoy.

Mule and rider showed in the red glow, directly in front of the only white-coated adobe building in town. The mule stood tracked underneath the large ridge log that jutted out ten feet from the front of the building. Captain Clay McCoy sat straight-backed in his saddle. There was a noose around the neck of the Ranger Captain, the long hangman's knot under one ear to twist his head a little sideways. Hatless, the shock of gray hair caught the red glow. The other end of the hangman's rope was tied to the ridge log. The Ranger Captain's arms were tied behind his back.

A mob of men surrounded the Ranger Captain and the mule, standing back a ways.

Most of them were Mexicans, penned in by a line of Aleman soldiers. Colonel Noel Guzman, sitting a played-out horse and holding a Luger in his hand, was shouting some sort of speech, but the words were lost in the blur of noise.

One Aleman soldier had a long blacksnake whip in his hands, and he was whipping the mule from behind. The mule's long ears were flattened back as he kicked with both hind feet.

Bass' hands were shaking as he raised his saddle carbine, but the hands of Pecos were steady as he lined his sights on the head of Noel Guzman and squeezed the trigger, the 30-30 slug tearing into the open mouth.

Bass spurred his horse before the dead Guzman hit the ground. He shot the soldier with the blacksnake. Every Texan had an Aleman soldier picked out, and they shot to kill. Bass had his knife in his hand as he rode alongside the blue mule. He cut the hangman's rope, then the rawhide thongs that bound the Ranger captain's arms. When Bass freed the noose, the flesh of the man's neck showed, raw and bleeding.

'The eternal God who made this mule put a soul in him,' the Ranger Captain's voice croaked. 'He'd have stood balked in his blessed tracks till they whipped him to death. I give thanks to God in that mule's name. I've been praying you'd show up, son. God has produced a miracle this night. He has used fire to cleanse this Mexican border, Aleman, Sodom and Gomorrah town. I have witnessed the working of God's hand this night.'

The Ranger Captain's face was gray, gaunt-looking, but there was a clarity to his eyes that defied exhaustion. When he saw Pecos, a slow grin spread under the grizzled mustache. 'Your sins are forgiven, you old rascal,' he said. 'And that goes for all you Texans.'

Somewhere beyond came the harsh voice of Colonel Baca. 'Viva! Viva Villa! Viva Yaqui! Viva Tejanos!' The Yaqui war cry filled the night.

'That'll be Colonel Baca of the army of Pancho Villa,' said Bass. 'There won't be an Ademan soldier left alive when he gets done mopping up.'

The Ranger Captain rubbed his raw neck. He spoke to the Mexicans. 'Take all the women and children across the river into Texas before the big battle starts here. Pronto!'

When they had gone, he spoke to Bass. 'Kate Crawford and her daughter are somewhere on this side of the river, Bass. Lobo Jones and his curly wolves are holding them for high ransom. That is what brought me across the river. Jones sucked me into this Aleman trap.'

'He's holding the women on Isla Diablo, sir,' Bass said quietly. 'With the arsenal and ammunition dump blown up and this town afire, there is no tellin' what that big renegade might do, if he gets scary. It simmers down to a one-man job,' Bass said grimly. 'And I'm the man for the job.'

'A two-man job,' the Ranger Captain corrected him. 'I'll side you.' He turned to Pecos. 'I'll thank you for the loan of your gun, Pecos. The Alemans took mine.'

CHAPTER ELEVEN

Isla Diablo was a spearhead that pointed sharply upstream, to split the current with a narrow sandbar that was barbed by rocks, sharp and cruel as the teeth of a shark. Sometimes in the early spring, the island was flooded, and only the tops of the high brush showed above the muddy surface. When the flood waters subsided, however, the island took shape. The sand and silt and debris were left between the sharp rocks, and for long weeks the island gave off the rotted stench of drowned carcasses of cattle and horses and the wildlife animals that lodged and lay buried in the black sand. Swamp tule grass sprouted from this rotted fertilizer, and the grass had a bitter taste. The leaves and a bank of the brush had the same bitterness. It was as if the island thrived on death.

There was a black sandbar at the wide end of the spearhead. The sides of the island were steep rocks, brush-coated, to make it impossible to climb the sheer wall. The water around the island was deep. The black sandbar gave off a phosphorescent shine on a dark night, like the glow of a damp sulphur match, or the glitter of quicksilver.

The sandbar was deceptive because it had a hard-packed look, but let a cowbrute, or a horse or a man set foot on the shiny black sand, and they would sink from sight in a matter of minutes in the quicksand. A man, familiar with the treachery of the deadly quicksand, could tell when Isla Diablo had swallowed meat and bone and was digesting its kill, because huge bubbles would slowly swell with a black phosphorescent metallic beauty to the size of a toy balloon. Then they would burst with an audible sound to free a noxious gas, and underneath the bubbling surface could be heard a strange rumbling, like the gurgle of a fat man's paunch after a heavy meal of indigestible food.

No man in his right mind, even if borracho drunk, would set foot on Isla Diablo, the Island of the Devil. Even Texans, given to boasting of their bravery, gave Isla Diablo a safe berth when they forded the Rio Grande.

For a man with a peculiar brand of intestinal fortitude, however, Isla Diablo made a good hideout. There were few, though, who cared for such sanctuary, preferring to risk capture or death. No human being this side of sanity wanted to live with the stench of rotting death clogging their nostrils.

It was rumored about that Isla Diablo had long been the hideout of El Lobo Jones. He had been known to brag that he was the only man alive who had lived there for days and weeks on end. Because it was impossible to ride a horse across the black quicksand, El Lobo went there by rowboat. He had either discovered or made a place to land along the high rocky side of the island. How he scaled the sheer slippery rocks was his own secret, and he kept that secret well.

The thought of Kate and Kit Crawford being held prisoners on the foul, stinking island, was hard to take. Neither man made mention of it when they forded the Rio Grande.

'Have you got some kind of a rowboat at Palofox?' Bass had asked as they reached the bank on the Texas side of the river.

'Two or three,' came the answer. 'But where in hell are you going to land on that stinkin' island?'

'I'll manage somehow.' Bass had been thinking about it, off and on, since Yaqui had told him where the two women were. 'We'll take along our reatas and a machete to cut out a trail, unless we're lucky enough to find where Lobo Jones' boat is tied up. He's bound to have a trail of some kind cut.'

'We've spotted smoke through field glasses from time to time,' said the Ranger Captain. 'Once or twice I sighted his campfire in the center of the island, where there seemed to be a clearing.'

'It's my guess that El Lobo has a trail on each side of the island, in case he has to make a fast getaway,' said Bass.

'In that case, we'd better use two boats. You come downstream on one side. I'll take the other, and we'll keep our boats hugging the sides. If we can time it right, we'll come up from opposite directions. We'll still have this dark to cover us till it gets daylight.' The Ranger Captain sounded hopeful.

'I think we got it, sir,' Bass agreed. 'All but the timing. We don't dare risk a shot that might booger that Lobo wolf. If we throw a scare into him, he'll do harm to the women.'

'Well have to chance it. You got a watch on you, Bass?'

Bass said he had. When they reached the Ranger Station and the young Ranger on duty sighted Captain Clay McCoy, he said, 'Good God!' as if it was a sort of prayer.

When the two men outlined their plan briefly to the Ranger, he said that Isla Diablo was closer to the Texas bank than to the Mexican side of the Rio Grande. 'You'll be on the soil of Texas, for all its stink, Cap. Some careless bastard threw that resignation you wrote out, in the stove. You're still a Captain in the Texas Rangers, Deacon!'

'You can give the careless bastard my vote of thanks. Take Bass' horse and my mule. Grain them and feed them all the hay they can eat. If you don't hear from me by sunrise, invade the island, regardless. Me'n' my son will be dead, so look for Kate Crawford and her daughter.'

They compared their watches as they shoved the two light skiffs into the river.

'We should be landed in half an hour,' said the Ranger Captain. 'It's a quarter past three. Let's make it four o'clock, son, to start up the trail.'

'Yes, sir,' came the quiet answer.

* * *

There was a dull glow touching the river to give the water the color of dark blood. The red glow shed across the metallic black surface of the sandbar, turning it into a sinister thing of spectacular beauty.

Bass had taken the south side of the island, and he steered the skiff dangerously close. He could see the large bubbles on the gunmetal sheen form slowly and then break to release the rotten stench. Then he noticed something riding there that did not belong there. He lifted it with an oar and dropped it into the skiff. It was a large felt Mexican sombrero with a silver Mexican eagle embroidered on the high crown. The last time Bass had seen the sombrero it was slanted at a caballero angle on the handsome head of young Pablo.

When the terrified scream came, Bass nearly let go his grip on the oars. Fighting back the nausea that slimed in his throat, he swung the prow of the skiff into the black sand. He grabbed the rawhide reata and shaking out a loop, he swung it. It fell over the head and shoulders of the man sunk waist deep in the sucking black quicksand.

'Quit hollerin', Pablo! Get the rope under your arms and hang on!' Bass tied the end of the reata to the ring that was bolted to the prow and put all his weight against the oars. For a time that seemed hours the skiff stood still, then slowly started moving to pull the bogged-down Pablo clear and out into the water. He was half-drowned when Bass hauled him into the boat. The young Mexican lay there, sobbing for breath.

'Lie quiet, Pablo. Make no noise!' Bass warned him.

'My caballo—! One of the golden horses—the gift of Dona Catalina, went into that black bog, screaming like a woman, Senor. Madre de Dios!'

'Make no sound, compadre!' Bass whispered the warning. 'Otherwise I will be forced to knock you senseless with an oar. Wash the muck off the best you can without upsetting the boat.'

'They told me Dona Catalina and the Senorita Kit were on this stinking Isla Diablo,' Pablo said. 'I came alone, thinking that the quicksand was but a lie that El Lobo had made up to scare anyone away. I had to get drunk enough to take the danger. It is no lie about the quicksand. Por Dios, my golden horse!' Pablo went silent as the skiff scraped rock.

Bass saw the rowboat tied to the rocky bank and swung the skiff alongside, making it fast to the other boat that was riding on a rope fastened to a heavy steel grappling hook, anchored to a jutting rock that surfaced the black water.

A ten-foot rocky cliff faced Bass, and he looked around for visible means to scale the slick-slimed surface. He saw a tree stump above. He roped it and pulled the rope slowly taut, testing it with his weight.

'I'm leaving you here, Pablo. You still got your fancy six-shooter?'

'Si, Senor. Fouled with slime.'

'Clean it up. Use it if El Lobo shows up. Don't miss!' Bass struck a match. The hands of his watch showed fifteen minutes past four. He was a quarter hour late.

Bass went up the rope, hand over hand, his feet climbing the black rock. When he gained the top of the high bank, he hunkered down, listening, breathing fast through his opened mouth. There was a rope ladder with small, stout, wooden rungs, tied to the tree stump. When he heard no sound and no one showed, he lowered the ladder and called down to Pablo in a cautious whisper.

'Stay down there with the boats.' Bass could make out the shadowy form of Pablo below. 'The ladder is for Dona Catalina and her daughter. Nobody else. Is that understood, compadre?'

'Si, Senor,' came the tense reply. 'I would go with you. I am no coward, but there is something fearsome being here alone in the dark. The smell of death is here, and I am afraid of that which cannot be seen. Take me with you, Tejano. Por favor!'

When Pablo tried to get to his feet, his legs gave way, and he bit back his sharp cry of pain. 'It is my legs,' he whimpered. 'Broken, I think.'

'Just stretched from the pull of the quicksand. Stay there, and be of use where you are. Hell, man, I can't carry you on my back. I'm late now. Quit crying. It's time to show some guts!'

Bass stiffened as he heard the explosion of a gun somewhere on the island. He crouched, breathing through his open mouth to hear better, but there was no answering shot. He could draw his own conclusion. Either the Ranger Captain had been killed, or he had killed Lobo Jones.

Bass groped till he found the narrow trail that had been hacked out through the high, dense brush thicket. He did his utmost to make no sound, but he made a hell of a racket in his own ears as he felt his way along, the thorny brush snagging at him like animal claws.

Bass had gone almost beyond earshot when Pablo called after him. He heard the call and shoved it away. Pablo had already delayed him too long. Let Pablo fight his own fear of the night and the smell of death. Bass' danger lay ahead, and he knew he was nearing it when he sighted the yellow glow of a campfire about a hundred yards ahead, filtering through the dense brush.

Bass crouched, trying to see movement against the yellow glow, every nerve taut now as he keyed his senses to catch the sound, sight or smell of the danger he felt all around him. The sudden crash of a heavy-caliber bullet, cannon-loud, as it ripped the silence, flattened Bass on his belly. He lay there, motionless, waiting for more shots or an outcry or groan, anything that usually follows a gunshot. There was nothing.

It had been like that first explosion of a bullet, sudden and without warning, and leaving an aftermath of stillness that was pregnant with danger. A man could read anything into those two separate shots, and keyed up as Bass was, he earmarked each shot as a separate murder. Quick and sudden and sure, leaving no ragged outcry, no dying moan, and there was the close feeling of danger if a man reached out for it.

Bass crawled on toward the yellow light where the gunshot had come from, moving with all the caution of a big-game hunter stalking a dangerous animal, the dismal thought prodding him on that somewhere on this stinking island was Kit and her mother and the big, loud-mouthed, tough and evil-minded, Lobo Jones.

Bass was thinking that if the first shot had killed the Ranger Captain and the second Kate Crawford, that would leave Kit at the mercy of the renegade. Those thoughts kept pounding at Bass, knifing his guts, burning him like a hot iron, sending him on at a snail's crawl when he should be there, should have been there long ago. It took all the will power and self-control he could summon up, to keep from charging it and getting the job done.

It seemed a hell of a long time before Bass came within actual sight of the place. He crouched low in the brush, with every sense alert as he reached a clearing no more than fifty feet in diameter. There were some slow-burning logs for a campfire that sent out a slim yellow glow. About a dozen feet back from the glow of the fire was what looked like an Indian hogan, a rounded mound of bent willows, caked and plastered over with hard-packed black mud. An old weather-stained wagon tarp covered the hogan. The entrance was horseshoe shaped, and even a half-grown boy or woman would have to crawl into the darkened doorway.

There was no sound at all around the empty clearing. No sign of life, save for the fire that a human hand had kindled. The campfire and the hogan had all the earmarks of a guntrap.

Bass crouched in the brush and waited for some sign of life. When the explosion of a .45 cartridge sounded, it caught Bass unprepared. Sparks flew in all directions from the campfire when the bullet had scattered coals in a red-hot shower.

Bass ducked instinctively, clamping his mouth down on a startled outcry. It looked like somebody had shot into the bonfire. Then a man's harsh voice came through the echoes of the explosion.

'How many times does a man have to warn you, you black-eyed bitch? What the hell you tryin' to do, tossin' cartridges into the fire? Signal the Rangers? Lobo Jones will show up any minute, wantin' to know what all the shootin's about. I'm comin' in there after you.' Brush broke as the man came into sight.

'Come back, you drunk fool,' another voice called out. 'You forget that the bossman said to keep out of the hogan?'

'She's got a belt full of cartridges. I don't know how in hell she flips 'em into the fire with her hands tied. Hell's fire, that racket will fetch the bossman here before he gets done digging up Guzman's money cache. Somebody's got to go in there and get the cartridges. She's hog-tied and gagged, so she can't holler for help.'

'Have at it, but I'm warning you right now, to stay outa that hut.'

'All I'm after is the shells.' The man was tall and lean, and his thick lips pulled back to show broken, yellow teeth. The man traveled like a skinny ape, his arms swinging below his knees.

Bass caught a split-second glimpse of the brass-shelled .45 bullets as if flipped from the dark doorway of the hogan into the hot coals and exploded just as the tall renegade stepped around the burning logs. Bass had his six-shooter cocked. His trigger finger jerked as the cartridge hit the fire. The man screamed as Bass' bullet caught him in the belly, staggering him a couple of steps before he went down, clawing at his belly. He doubled up and commenced rolling around on the ground, screaming and cursing. Bass' shot and the exploded cartridge had blended as one shot.

Bass saw the other man dart out from the brush with a knife in hand. The wounded man did not see the knife till it slit his throat.

The second man was short and wiry, pale-eyed. A week's stubble of dirty yellow whiskers gave him a mangy look. He wiped the blood from his knife on the dead man's dirty overalls and shoved it into a leather scabbard. He went through the dead man's pockets with the deft, swift skill born of long practice. His bowed legs and wiry build and the quick way he had of moving marked him for an ex-jockey.

Bass had his thumb on the hammer of his six-shooter when he heard a man call from the brush behind the hogan.

'What you got in mind, fella?' The quiet drawl belonged to Ranger Captain Clay McCoy.

The little renegade snarled something as he made a dive for the doorway of the hogan. The heavy .45 slug from the Ranger Captain's gun hit the crown of his sweat-marked hat, shattering the skull.

'Better hurry, son,' the Ranger Captain called. 'They're on their way. This will fetch them.' He dragged the dead man by the feet to clear the doorway and went into the hogan.

Bass reckoned he meant Lobo Jones and the rest of his renegades, and that the shooting would bring them. He was there at the doorway when Kit came crawling out. He pulled her onto her feet and held her close and tight in his arms. There was a dry sob in her throat when she reached up to kiss him. Kate Crawford came out on her hands and knees, with the Ranger Captain's help.

'Kit and I were anxious about Bass in the hands of the Yaquis and were foolish enough to cross into Mexico alone,' Kate Crawford explained. 'We were at the mercy of El Lobo.'

Bass took the guns from the holsters of the

dead men and handed one to Kate Crawford. She slid it into the empty holster that hung from her cartridge belt.

'I had a struggle getting the cartridges from my belt with my hands tied, but I managed to flip them into the fire. I knew you'd come, Clay, you and Bass. I warned you the only way I could that you were walking into a gun-trap.'

'You did all right, Kate,' Clay McCoy told her. 'Did Lobo Jones hurt you or Kit?'

'He hasn't had time,' Kate said grimly. 'And he gave his renegades orders not to manhandle us or he'd kill them.'

'You got here just in time,' Kit said, and Bass felt her shudder against his shoulder. 'Those two hombres have been taking it out in talking.' Kit's voice was a harsh whisper.

They were back in the dark shadow of the brash now.

'My skiff is on the north side of the island, tied alongside Lobo's rowboat,' said the Ranger Captain. 'Where'd you tie up, Bass?'

'Alongside his other boat on the south side. I left Pablo in the skiff,' said Bass.

'Pablo?' chorused both women.

'Yeah. Pulled him out of the quicksand at the spearhead. He's in no shape to travel. He's got his gun and his knife, and there's a carbine in the skiff. I told him to wait. But he's shore spooky. He was givin' up head when I left, but I didn't wait to hear what he said.'

'If he looked in the rowboat,' Kate

Crawford said, 'he'd find the money there. It's in waterproof metal boxes. It's Jefe Guzman's money that's been buried on this foul-smelling island, in deep pockets at the spearhead beside the quicksand. Lobo's been working there since dark, and he told me he'd have the last box loaded before daybreak. Then he'd take Kit along in his boat, and he'd drop me on the Texas bank near the Ranger headquarters at Palofox.

'It would be up to me,' she said, 'to hold the Texas Rangers back until Lobo Jones got away. If they followed him, he'd make it tough on Kit. But if I held them back, he'd release Kit, unharmed, for a high ransom he said I could afford to pay. He was to let me know later where the payoff would take place.

'El Lobo has Guzman's money in his boat on the south side of the island, but half of the twelve renegades he has here with him would have to use the boat he has tied on the north side, so they would either have to draw lots or fight to see who went in El Lobo's boat. He figures on them fighting it out, and while they were doing battle, he'd make his getaway, taking us and the money with him.'

'He'd have his hands full,' said the Ranger Captain.

'Lobo Jones or any of his men haven't come to find out what the shootin' was all about,' said Bass. 'I figure there was a third man bushed up. He laid low and then slipped off to take the news to Lobo. There's only one trail cut through to each boat. By now El Lobo has his men hid along both trails. Either trail we take now, we'd run into a bushwacker trap.'

'That's right,' said the Ranger grimly. 'We'll be better off to bush up and wait. I figure Jones and his renegades will drift off the island now, and fast, and not try to take their prisoners.'

Bass was worried about Pablo, but he kept his thoughts to himself. The two women sat on the ground, close together. Bass and the Ranger stood beside them, their guns in their hands.

They could hear the wind coming through the brush before they felt it. It sounded to Bass like the hissing rattle of the Yaquis as they stampeded the cattle. It was an east wind that came up the river, and it came with a rush now, fanning the red coals of the campfire into flames, whipping the live coals skyward to fall in the brush thicket.

The two women were on their feet now, backing away from the blazing coals. In a few minutes the dry brush had caught fire, sweeping with a widening swathe toward the spearhead point of Isla Diablo. Through the roar of the flames could be heard the hoarse screams of men, trapped in the wide path of the brush fire.

Then the wind swirled crazily, and they took off their hats and slapped the chunks of coals from each other. Bass ran to the hogan and jerked off the wagon tarp. Ripping it in four pieces, they covered themselves like so many blanket-wrapped Indians. For a while they were in a corral of flames, then the men beat a wide path, and they followed in behind the fire, walking on the hot ashes of the burned-over ground. They angled toward the south side of the island. The soles of their boots felt terribly hot, but nobody complained.

Bass was in the lead when they came to the river bank. The heavy brush was burned to the ground. The rowboat and skiff were no longer there. Bass could see the charred remnant of the tree stump and rope ladder.

The small island was on fire now. The wind whipped ashes high into the air. The river was a blood color under the heavy smoke pall. Chunks of black embers floated on the surface, and what looked like a waterlogged tree floated slowly. The log came to a stop and swung broadside to the current, and Pablo's voice came cautiously from below.

'I released the rowboat from its anchor chain and shoved it into the current. I took the skiff quietly upstream and watched the fire.' Pablo stood up amid the brush he had used for a clever camouflage.

'Hold the skiff steady, Pablo.' Bass called to him. 'We are lowering Dona Catalina and Kit into the skiff.'

There was enough of the rawhide reata left

to fasten under the arms of both women. While Pablo kept the skiff close to the rocky wall, the two women were lowered into it. Three people was the skiff's capacity.

'Shove off, Pablo,' the Ranger Captain called down. 'Land at Palofox. Pronto, man!'

'What of you, Senor Bass?' Pablo called up. 'If there is fighting to be done, I will gladly take your place, Bassito.'

'Sit down, Pablo,' Bass called down, 'before you upset the boat. I am grateful for your gesture of bravery. Gracias, companero! But my place is here with my father. Hurry! The curly wolves are coming. Pronto, man, if you value the lives of Dona Catalina and her daughter. Pronto, and in silence!'

The skiff, with the three passengers under the brush camouflage, slid downstream and into the sluggish channel; to drift like a waterlogged tree with the whim of the current. It made a shapeless black blot on the smoky-red water. There was no dip of oars, no creaking sound of oarlocks. Pablo was letting the current drag the skiff downstream. There was no movement, no sign of life on the shapeless blot.

The Ranger Captain and Bass were crouched low, almost flat on the burnt ground, and the heat from the warm ashes and charred wood was bringing out the sweat. They were watching half a dozen of Lobo Jones' renegades as they prowled the high, rocky bank of the island for a glimpse of the rowboat. A pair of them were watching the black blot as it drifted slowly downstream.

'Hell, it's nothin' but a waterlogged tree,' one renegade said. 'But who the hell stole the boat? It didn't slip that anchor chain by itself.'

'Mebbyso the bossman taken it.'

'Dios hombre!' The voice of Pablo, not loud, but with a clarity that carried across the hundred yards of water. 'There were many boxes of metal, all padlocked, in that big rowboat of El Lobo's, that I released from the anchor chain and set adrift. Only things of high value are deserving of a strong padlock but I did not have time to see what was in them. The voices of men were approaching, and there was hardly time to free the boat. One wonders what was in the metal boxes—'

Bass bit back a gritty groan as Pablo's words drifted back to the island from the camouflaged skiff.

'I'm a sonofobitch!' one of the pair cursed. 'You hear what I heard? That ain't no floating tree.' He lifted his carbine and was lining his sights when the Ranger Captain's gun spat flame. The renegade screamed and went down. Bass shot his companion who had his gun raised to his shoulder.

Bass and the Ranger Captain lay flat on their bellies now. It took a few minutes before the four remaining outlaws, who had been listening to Pablo's words, became aware of this new threat. They stared in stupid bewilderment at their two companions, who lay dead on the ground.

'This is it, son!' the Ranger Captain gritted. 'Shoot fast, and don't miss.' The crack of his saddle gun punctuated his orders.

Bullets kicked hot ashes into Bass' face and eyes. Red pain stabbed his eyes, and he squeezed them shut against the hot, flaky ashes. He pried them open against the pain and pointed his carbine at the moving black shadow of a man and pulled the trigger. He heard the man's yelp of pain as bullets kicked chunks of burning ashes into his face. The ground was as hot as a cook stove against his belly.

'It's that Ranger Captain!' hollered one of El Lobo's renegades. 'And that Bass Texican bastard! Shorty seen 'em shoot the jockey and his pardner. Let's kill the sonsabitches!'

Bass pointed his gun blindly at the sound of the voice and commenced shooting as fast as he could lever cartridges into the breech of his 30-30 saddle carbine. He kept squinting the red pain from his eyes, forcing them open long enough to catch the black outline of a man. When his carbine went empty, Bass reached for his six-shooter.

'Looks like we finished 'em off, son,' Clay McCoy's voice was gritty. 'No use wastin' good bullets.'

'This Devil's Island,' Bass said as he got to

his feet, slapping hot ashes from his shirt that was scorched and burned in a few places. 'It's shore named right for hot chunks. You hurt, Cap"n?'

'I'm sittin' on a good bed of barbecue coals right now. I could use a hand up, with this rump roast I got in the seat of my pants.'

Bass could make his father out through the red haze that filmed his eyes. He reached a hand down and pulled the older man slowly to his feet. The Ranger Captain stood hip-shot with his weight on one leg, using the carbine for a short crutch. His other hand gripped Bass' shoulder.

'Take a feller my age.' The Ranger spoke with an unconcerned tone. 'His bones get brittle. A danged steel-jacket bullet splintered my shin bone, just above my boottop. I got a rag twisted tight to stop the blood. See can you find a bare place where there are no roastin' coals. I feel kinda like sittin' down.'

They sat on a bare rock, side by side. Bass used the Ranger's black silk neck handkerchief, wet with the blood from his leg wound, to wipe his eyes.

'There'll be a boatload of Texas Rangers along, directly,' Clay McCoy said. 'We might as well take it easy till the boys get here.'

A keening cry that was almost a scream, shattered the silence.

'Help! Help!' The hoarse, agonized cry came from the spearhead point of the island.

'Lobo Jones!' said the Ranger Captain.

'El Lobo, caught in his own slimy trap.' Bass' voice was without mercy.

'Help! Gawdamighty, help!'

'Who is he to ask help from God?' Bass stood, legs spread, staring into the night with half-blinded eyes.

'He is a voice crying in the wilderness.' It was Deacon Clay McCoy who now spoke. 'A human voice, in the form of a man created in God's image.'

'Lobo Jones has shoved men into that black bog.' Bass spoke harshly. 'He has bragged about it.'

Bass had his six-shooter in his hand. 'If you hear a shot,' Bass called back as he started walking toward the spearhead, 'you'll know I got chicken-hearted and put El Lobo Jones outa his misery.'

CHAPTER TWELVE

The fire had gutted the island of brush, leaving only the charred stumps showing like black tombstones in a graveyard. There were scattered patches of live coals that filmed an angry red across the blackened ground. Bass could make it all out now. He could now make out the phosphorescent glow on El Lobo's black-slimed body as he floundered around in a terrified effort to break free from the quicksand that sucked his legs down. Bass' half-blinded eyes could not see the six-shooter in the shoulder holster because the holster was black, and the butt of the gun was black.

When the trapped renegade sighted Bass walking slowly across the burnt ground and saw the carbine cradled in Bass' arm, he knew that Bass had come to watch him die a slow death or shoot him.

Lobo Jones slid his gun out, taking care to keep it close to him so that it would not be seen at that distance. He shoved the gun barrel into his mouth and licked and sucked the stinking muck off, spitting it out before it gagged him with nausea. He fingered the muck out of the shoulder holster and slid the gun back in and up under his armpit, and waited for Bass to come within range.

He would beg for his life, cry and beg and grovel to the man he hated. He looked at his maimed right hand that was a misshapen claw. Bass had done that to him the night he shot the bottle from his hand. The hand was in constant pain. All he had to do was clench it shut, and the memory of what Bass had done came back. He watched Bass coming, and hate overrode his terror of death.

Bass had to move slowly. The whole ground ahead was black to the spearhead, with the brush gone. Bass could not tell where the solid ground left off and the quicksand bog commenced. All of it was blanketed with ashes. His teeth bared when he halted fifty feet from the black quicksand.

Lobo Jones had thought up a hundred pleas for mercy and discarded them all, because in the plea for his life he would have to have something that would appeal to Bass Slocum.

'There's a seventy-five foot reata,' Lobo said, breaking the heavy silence, 'tied to that stump where you're standing. I've been using it to pull myself out of the deep holes where Jefe Guzman and me hid some strongboxes, but them dirty, double-crossin' curly wolves of mine snaked the rope back while I was fishin' out the last of the boxes, and ducked from sight. I hollered, but nobody answered. They left me here to die. I was here alone when the brush fire started. Three, four of 'em got trapped and headed back. They had to wade in or be burned to death. I had the satisfaction of watchin' those bastards die. Their screams was shore sweet music—

'When the fire burned over I tried to pull myself out, lost my handhold and slipped into the bog, and I started yelling for help.

'There's twenty-five of those little strongboxes,' he said, bluster creeping into his voice. 'Ten thousand dollars in each box. It's all yours if you throw me that rope. Two hundred and twenty-five thousand dollars, Bass. I'll tell you where to find it, if you throw the rope.'

'We already got it,' Bass said flatly.

'You're lyin'!' the trapped man screamed hoarsely.

'No need to lie to a dyin' man.' Bass laid his carbine on the ground and rolled a cigarette and lit it. He picked up the coiled reata that was crusted with black muck that had dried, but the rawhide had not burned and was still pliable. Bass shook a loop and tried spinning it. He gave it up with a grin.

'I seen a trick roper once keep one goin' in each hand and one in his teeth. You got to have a knack for it and plenty practice.' Bass spoke casually, coiling the rope and dropping it on the ground.

Bass took his watch out to read the time. 'I reckon you'll never see sunrise,' Bass said and left it like that, putting the watch back in his pocket.

Lobo Jones tried playing it from another angle. 'They tell me that Captain Clay McCoy preaches the funeral sermons of the men he kills.'

'That's right,' said Bass.

'Is he goin' to preach over them dirty double-crossin' renegades of mine that you and he killed?'

'I reckon.'

'I'd like for him to come over here. I've been a sinful man, and I'm scared to die because I'm bound for hell, but if Deacon McCoy was to come here and say a prayer it might help make 'er an easy crossin'.'

'Mebby.' Bass got slowly to his feet.

'You'll fetch the Deacon?'

'Hell, no.' Bass stubbed out his cigarette. 'You got a hell of a memory when it comes to forgettin' things you don't want to remember, but I ain't forgot about the screw-worms you planned to let eat my brains out. I've been thinkin' things over since I got here. I came to watch you die, but somehow I ain't got the stummick for it.'

Bass picked up the reata and shook a loop. 'The screamin' and beggin' and slobberin' you'd put yourself through would make me puke, so I'm goin' to drag you out, let you dry off and get organized. Then I'll stake you to my saddle gun and give you a chance for your taw.' Bass swung the loop around to loosen the mud-caked crust, leaving the end of the rope tied to the burned-over tree stump.

'Hold your arms up,' Bass called as he pitched the loop across the black bog. It was a sure loop that settled down over Lobo Jones' upraised arms and around his chest. As Bass jerked the loop tight it caught in the holstered gun. Lobo Jones grabbed the gun as it slid from the holster.

The trapped man's brain worked with split-second swiftness, thinking. The other end of the reata was tied hard and fast to the tree stump, and he could use it to pull himself free of the bog. In a fair gun duel, in his played-out condition, he knew he would be no match for Bass Slocum. As the slippery gun came into his hand, he thumbed the hammer back. It was a point-blank fifty-foot range. He could not miss. He jerked the trigger.

Bass knew from the bent-over position of the man that he held the gun in his hand. The whine of the bullet was in Bass' ears when Jones fired. His half-blinded eyes cleared enough to see the mud and shattered skull bone splatter like a rock thrown into a thick mud puddle. Lobo Jones lay sprawled on his belly, his face in the mud, his arms outflung.

Bass had no wish to watch the grisly ending. He turned away. He now watched the slack in the reata slowly tighten and the burned-over end of the rope around the tree stump weaken and break away. Then he walked slowly back to where he had left his foster-father.

The Ranger Captain was no longer alone. Two men were with him. One of the men started walking toward Bass. It was Pecos.

'A day late and a dollar short.' Pecos spoke disgustedly. 'Us fellers had 'er made to invade this stinkin' island. Got picked up by the Rangers. I came up with one Ranger, an' the others stayed below in the boat. Cap'n McCoy tied the rope we threw him to a tree stump an' we climbed up the rope.' Pecos motioned at the dead man.

'How did you make out, son?' The Ranger Captain questioned Bass as they came up.

'Lobo Jones had it made to kill me and haul himself out of the bog by the rope I threw him. He didn't quite make it.'

'You been tryin' for a long time, Pecos,' Captain Clay McCoy spoke gently, 'to make a dicker for you and your Texans to come back to Texas. You'll get your chance now, and I'll make sure you all get a fair trial.'

Bass Slocum McCoy was tried in a Texas law court for the killing of the drunk and quarrelsome stranger who had killed a Texas Ranger and was wearing the dead Ranger's shirt. The jury cleared Bass without leaving the box.

Within an hour after the trial, the Ranger Captain had administered the oath of allegiance and handed Bass and the other prodigal sons of Texas their commissions in the Texas Rangers.

When the Ranger Captain had gone, Bass broke the empty silence. 'Gentle Annies,' Bass faced the Texans. 'Did it ever occur to you that, a while back things were in one hell of a mess, and it took a top hand like God to straighten things out? One of his reps just went out that door.'

The propaganda pamphlets and all details regarding the Aleman Plan were on their way to the War Department at Washington, D.C., to be placed on file. The town of Alemanda was completely destroyed. Colonel Baca had left to take up his duties in the Villista army, and Yaqui was taking his Yaquis back to their stronghold in the hills, having refused to accept the offer of the Santa Catalina Rancho. Pancho Villa had sent word by Colonel Baca for Dona Catalina to move her Mexicans back to the grant which the Villistas would leave unharmed.

Pablo and Pepita were married in Mexico. Pepita had given her knife to the grizzled Pecos, telling Pablo she had just been teasing him. Pablo was to remain as Major Domo of the Santa Catalina Rancho.

There was a big barbecue taking place at the Big C Ranch in Texas in celebration of the double wedding of Kate Crawford to Ranger Captain Clay McCoy, and Kit Crawford to Ranger Bass Slocum McCoy.

We hope you have enjoyed this Large Print book. Other Chivers Press or Thorndike Press Large Print books are available at your library or directly from the publishers.

For more information about current and forthcoming titles, please call or write, without obligation, to:

Chivers Large Print
published by BBC Audiobooks Ltd
St James House, The Square
Lower Bristol Road
Bath BA2 3SB
UK
email: bbcaudiobooks@bbc.co.uk
www.bbcaudiobooks.co.uk

OR

Thorndike Press
295 Kennedy Memorial Drive
Waterville
Maine 04901
USA
www.gale.com/thorndike
www.gale.com/wheeler

All our Large Print titles are designed for easy reading, and all our books are made to last.